The Monksford Inc

To the friends who saved my life without realising it.

*"Shooting stars and healing scars,
Skin and bone and coming home."*

One.

Doctor Morgan Black's return to Monksford went entirely unnoticed, at first. Although, in time, it would change everything. The driver who brought him from Newton station didn't recognise him and tactfully realised his customer did not wish to engage in small talk, a fact which earned him a generous tip. Morgan did not recognise the owner of the bed and breakfast but the way she glanced at him from time to time as she dealt with another guest made Morgan wonder if she knew him. He checked into the modest lodgings at eight in the evening, took a hot shower to wash away some of the fatigue of over thirty-six hours of travel and retired to his room, not emerging until breakfast the next morning where he grazed on two poached eggs on toast and a cup of tea whilst reading the manuscript for a book on African folklore, which he had been asked to write a foreword for.

Morgan returned to his room and attempted to cobble together a suitable outfit from the clothes in his suitcase. He settled on some dark trousers and a shirt and blazer combination that had been out of fashion for almost a decade. He attempted to comb his mop of brown hair with little success and made his way downstairs, leaving his key at reception before heading out into the morning sunshine.

His intention was to take a walk through the nearby Corley Woods but he was advised by a passer-by that recent heavy rains had flooded the path so opted to visit the churchyard instead, where he studied the familiar Norman stonework for a time. Morgan stopped short of entering the church and sat on a damp bench underneath a tree and watched the magpies hopping from grave to grave in the soft morning sunlight.

When the hour of his appointment neared, he took the riverside path towards a small shopfront where a faded gold on green sign read 'E.R. Erwig - Solicitors'. He entered and was quickly shown into an office, where a man in his early sixties dressed in an impossibly immaculate suit stood to greet him.
'Doctor Black, I assume?'
Morgan cringed internally as he shook the proffered hand wondering whether this phrase was a reference to his extensive time in Africa or a simple pleasantry.
'Morgan is fine, it's a pleasure to meet you Mr Erwig.'
The solicitor offered Morgan a large comfortable chair in front of the great oak desk and sat himself down in a larger, even more comfortable chair behind it.

Morgan was struck by how much Mr Erwig resembled a Dickens' character when he removed his glasses, with small eyes, a large nose and hair that had obviously been dyed black. His facial appearance made him look a serious and austere man, in sharp contrast to his warm smile and friendly demeanour.

'Please, call me Eric. Let us dispense with the formalities, your aunt was a friend of mine and I assisted her when she became your guardian. You were just a child, of course, and probably don't remember.'

Morgan looked at his feet and momentarily felt like a child again instead of a doctor of anthropology, 'I have some recollection.'

'Let me start by offering my condolences, your aunt was an incredible and inspiring woman and, as I said, a good friend of mine. I am sorry that news did not reach you in time for you to attend the funeral.'

Morgan recovered his composure enough to politely thank the gentleman sat opposite him.

'Your Aunt Eliza was well thought of in the village; a prominent member of the local history society; a regular speaker at the Women's Institute and a friendly face at many village events. She will be missed. She was very proud of you, Morgan, and your work. I know you wrote to her as often as you were able and she was always keen to let people know how your travels were going. We tried to hold off on the funeral but it becomes difficult after a time. I am sorry. If it is any consolation, she had everything planned and it was a beautiful tribute to a great woman.'

'Thank you, that's good to know.'

'As for the matter of the will,' Erwig continued, glancing at the papers in front of him, 'Your aunt's academic career brought her a fair income. She lived within her means and amassed some savings, as well as her cottage and antique collection. There are a few small legacies, a donation to the history society, the RSPB and a gift for Mr and Mrs Cartwright, her neighbours, who cooked and cleaned for her and maintained her garden when she became unable. Everything else she has left to you. She writes that she looks upon you as if you were her own child and that she is proud of the man you have become.'

Morgan's hazel eyes filled with tears, 'Thank you. She was a wonderful person.'

The solicitor pushed forward a box of paper tissues he produced from somewhere.

'She was.'

After his meeting with the solicitor Morgan walked across the village to Mr and Mrs Cartwright's house for his second appointment of the day. The doctor sat at their kitchen table while Mrs Cartwright,

Cathy, insisted on making him lunch and chatted incessantly at him about his aunt, how good a woman she was and how proud she was of Morgan. Mr Cartwright, Tom, sat quietly drinking cup after cup of tea and flicking through the newspaper, occasionally attempting to add some detail to one of his wife's stories before being interrupted.

Morgan had known the Cartwrights since he moved to his aunt's house as a boy and he'd always known that Mr Cartwright was a quiet man but the thought only now occurred to him that it was because he could never get a word in edgeways. The couple had always been old to Morgan, but Cathy seemed thinner and paler than he remembered and Tom had less hair and more wrinkles.

It was a pleasant enough afternoon, even if he had little interest in the adventures of Mrs Jenson's cat, Doctor Black was pleased to hear some stories about Eliza that he'd never heard before, some because they were so recent and some because they were so old.

'Martha and Harry got married last Spring,' Mrs Cartwright continued, 'and they're expecting their first baby any day now. Do you remember little Jimmy Smith? The butcher's son, you used to play together when you were young.'

Morgan nodded lazily as Mrs Cartwright continued to list half a decade's worth of comings and goings. 'Well, he's moved up north somewhere, working for British Rail – or what is left of it. Young Simon is back from university, doing well I hear. Shirley and Ken broke up, she's living on St Peter's Close now. Her sister is off somewhere.'

The clock in the hallway chimed three and, as she had each hour before, Mrs Cartwright exclaimed, 'Is that the time?'. Mr Cartwright declared that he was going to the pub. Although Morgan turned down Tom's offer to join him, he did take the opportunity to suggest that he too should be leaving. It was another half an hour before he was able to leave with the key to his aunt's house.

He contemplated heading straight over but decided to delay such a potentially painful task until the morning, instead choosing to take a walk downriver from the village towards Prince's Wood, which he had explored many times in his youth, before returning to his lodgings for a light dinner and the final few chapters of the book on African folklore.

It was in fact two days later that Morgan finally entered his aunt's house for the first time in five years. In the intervening time he took trips on the bus to Newton to re-register at the library, purchase some new shoes and visit his Aunt's grave. He also took numerous walks in Prince's Wood and at one point even contemplated visiting the village pub, The Devil's Due, but decided he couldn't face that yet either.

When he finally found himself devoid of further excuses, he walked through the village to the cottage, where he stood in the garden for several long minutes admiring Mr Cartwright's handywork. Just as he was about the head inside, he heard the neighbouring cottage's door swing open and the voice of Mrs Cartwright emanate from the porch.

'They've been up on the heath every night this week, making fires and all sorts,' she was explaining to her husband.

'Who has?' said Mr Cartwright as he stepped out onto the path.

'Yobs. They've got nothing better to do than cause trouble.'

'It's just boys being boys,' Tom replied, before glancing over at Morgan and rolling his eyes.

'I saw that!' Mrs Cartwright declared, 'Who's out there?'

She emerged from the hallway, the stern look on her face turning into a big smile when she saw Morgan.

'Oh, Morgan. Good afternoon! How are you? Old Mrs. Green from the shop said that she saw you in town yesterday'

Mr Cartwright tactfully interrupted his wife, 'I'm off then.' He whistled and Bruce, his ever-loyal spaniel, emerged from the house to follow his master down the garden path.

'He taking Bruce for a walk?' Morgan enquired.

'Don't you believe it,' Mrs Cartwright replied, 'He's off down the pub.'

After a slightly protracted conversation about village affairs, Mrs Cartwright returned to her housework and Morgan was finally able to head inside. The first thing he noticed was the smell of stale air and old books. Mrs Cartwright had given the place a dust and vacuum a few days before, in preparation for his arrival and the entire house was clean and tidy with everything in its proper place – just the way he remembered it. The smell, however, was all wrong. No fresh flowers; no faint traces of Aunt Eliza's perfume; nothing cooking in the kitchen. The odour was more reminiscent of the archives of his old university than of his childhood home. He found himself thinking about Howard Carter's diary, which he'd read in his youth, and how the famous Egyptologist recalled the stale scent of time on first opening Tutankhamen's tomb. Morgan pushed the thought aside; he must not think of this place as a tomb –

this was his Aunt's home and had once been his home too. Instead, he walked through the small house, opening every window and door and pulling back every curtain, filling the place with light and fresh air.

He lingered in the living room for a long time. Above the fireplace, there were pictures of Eliza's friends and family and chief among them, in the very centre was a picture of him and his Aunt outside the Dome of the Rock in Jerusalem. The frame sat on top of a copy of Morgan's book on ancient fertility cults, elevating the picture above the others. This symbol of his Aunt's pride in him filled his eyes with tears and he retreated back into the hallway.

He hesitated at the closed door to his Aunt's room, his hand hovering over the handle. He stepped back and decided that this was a challenge for tomorrow. Instead, he went upstairs and into his old room and sat on the bed for several long minutes before looking through the cupboards and drawers in wonder at possessions he'd forgotten he'd ever owned: an old atlas, long out of date; some once beloved vinyl records and an old notepad full of the thoughts and sketches of his teenage self.

Hunger roused Morgan from his memories, as did the cool evening wind blowing through the house. He closed all the windows and doors and drew all the curtains, pleased that the stale odour had departed. He stopped at the door to each room he'd entered to survey the seemingly impossible task of sorting through the contents of the house, even though he didn't know what he planned to do with it. Finally, after turning out the last light, he locked the front door behind him and walked out into the cool night air.

The cottage sat down an old country lane, not far from the village centre. With the exception of the farmhouse next-door, it was the furthest house from the hub of Monksford where the village shops, the church and Morgan's bed and breakfast were located. It had been a great spot to spend his youth, with plenty of fields and woods to explore and many local legends to learn about. As he walked, he recalled in his mind the great tales of witch trials and haunted woods that had thrilled him as a boy, alongside the region's role in the English Civil War and the battle that had taken place on the nearby heathland.

Morgan chuckled to himself at the sight of Mr Cartwright stumbling down the lane, presumably on his way back from the pub, accompanied by his faithful spaniel Bruce, who was now looking old and weary. Tom grinned at the site of Morgan and stopped when they reached each other.

'Good evening,' the old man said.

'Evening,' Morgan replied.

'Heading back to digs?'

'Yes,' the doctor said with a smile as he bent down to pet Bruce, 'How was the pub?'

'Still there, still there. Though I feel it will be my duty to check up on it tomorrow, just in case,' Mr Cartwright replied with a smile, 'Did she keep you long after I left?'

'Not long,' Morgan replied, 'I think she felt dutybound to tell me about each of Monksford's comings and goings in my absence.'

Tom nodded knowingly, 'Just remember,' he said with a sparkle in his eye, 'Mrs Cartwright doesn't know about everything that happens in Monksford.'

The old man turned from Morgan and continued down the lane, the old dog following closely behind him. 'Goodnight,' Morgan called out. The old man raised his hand, smiled and disappeared into the darkness.

Two.

Over the course of the next few days Morgan Black developed something of a routine. In the mornings he would eat breakfast at his bed and breakfast and then perform any errands, either in Monksford or Newton, including buying lunch and dinner for the day, or take a walk in Prince's Woods. He would then go to Aunt Eliza's house, eat some lunch and spend the afternoon sorting. Sorting mostly consisted of moving objects into piles and moving piles into boxes. However, he seemed to spend equally as much time emptying boxes into piles and moving objects between piles. Morgan would make himself a simple dinner, return to 'sorting' for a few more hours before walking back to the lodgings, where he would retire to his room to read before bed. Other than saying 'morning' to the occasional passer-by, regardless of the time of day, and exchanging pleasantries with shopkeepers, he spoke to almost no one for the best part of three days. He was perfectly happy keeping to himself, avoiding the demons of his past and giving him plenty of space for reflection.

On the third day of working on his aunt's house and his sixth day back in Monksford, Morgan's solitude finally broke. He was in the village shop, picking up some lunch, when old Mrs

Green became the first person to say more than three words to him in over forty-eight hours. Morgan didn't recognise her at first, but she recognised him instantly.

'Hello young Morgan. Off to University soon?'

'Hello ma'am,' Morgan replied, 'I got my PHD five years ago.'

'Oh good,' the old lady responded, 'How is your aunt?'

The shopkeeper, a lady in her late 50s with a kind face, interrupted, placing a hand on the old lady's arm, 'Liza died, Mrs Green. You were at her funeral. Do you remember?'

'Yes, dear and who is this?'

'This is Morgan, her nephew.' The shopkeeper gave Morgan an apologetic look.

Mrs Green looked up at Morgan, 'Have you seen the men in the crater?' she asked, 'It will be that time of year again soon.'

Morgan frowned and look at the shopkeeper who just shrugged and shepherded the old lady towards the counter to pay for her groceries.

After finishing his shopping, Morgan walked to his aunt's house, where Mrs Cartwright caught him at her garden gate and compelled him inside for a cup of tea. When she pressed him on his progress with the house, he admitted that he was struggling but turned down her offer to help him. When he finally made it to the cottage that evening, after dining with the Cartwrights, he resolved to enter his aunt's room.

Like the rest of the house, the room was much as he had remembered it – the memories now shrouded by a thin layer of dust. The bed was made; bottles lined the dresser; books filled the shelves and the writing desk was dominated by a small pile of notebooks. He could almost see his aunt sat there preparing a lecture or working on her latest piece of research. The only evidence that she had become infirm were her walking frame resting behind the door and the creak of plastic as Morgan sat on the bed. Tears filled his eyes and guilt racked his soul at the thought of having been away for so long. She had taken him in as a child when there was nowhere else, yet when she grew old and fell ill, he was halfway across the globe. Opportunities to speak had been rare since he left and in the last eighteen months completely impossible, but if only he'd known he would have come home in an instant; perhaps that is why she never divulged the true extent of her illness.

Morgan let out a sigh and watched the dust dance around the lightbulb. His eyes fell on Eliza's desk and the stack of notebooks. Had his aunt been working on something when she died? She'd made no mention of any writing project when they last spoke, she had been enjoying her retirement. Perhaps she had dug out some old notes for a WI talk or some other local event. Curiosity took Morgan across the room where he picked up the top notebook, a large hardcover black writing pad; blowing the dust from the cover he opened it carefully. Inside, in Eliza's methodical style, were notes from various sources compiled in some detail. Morgan recognised the format instantly and from the dates in the margins could tell that Eliza had indeed been heavily engaged in research when she died.

The book contained about fifteen pages of intense notes, dated up until a week before she had passed. He knew his aunt's methods well and recognised that these notes represented the last stage before the production of a full manuscript. The other, smaller notepads contained rough notes from various sources, some just a title and a page number or a few words or a name and were mostly meaningless to anyone but Eliza.

Morgan spent several hours leafing through the various notepads, books and pieces of paper spread across the desk and by the time he thought about returning to his lodgings he realised the front door had been long locked. Rather than return and wake up the landlady, he decided to sleep in his old room, in the bed Mrs Cartwright had made up before his arrival.

The next morning, Morgan moved his single suitcase out of the bed and breakfast and into his aunt's house, where he planned to stay for the immediate future while he sorted everything out.

Over the next two days, by cross-referencing Eliza's notes with various books, between futile attempts to sort, Morgan was able to determine that his aunt was preparing to write a book on the history of Monksford and the surrounding region. It seemed that her involvement in the local historical society had piqued her interest in the subject and, after a life of lecturing and writing important texts on medieval Britain, she decided to write one more book about Monksford.

As well as being his legal guardian from the age of ten, Aunt 'Liza had been his inspiration. He became obsessed with history as a teenager and would go on to pursue a career in academia that would lead to him becoming an expert on ancient fertility cults, with a book to his name that had allowed him to travel to other parts of the world to speak at universities and visit famous sites used in the worship of Cybele, Oshun, Bastet, Quetzalcoatl and others. Morgan enjoyed his work and had always been grateful for the opportunities it had opened up for him. He was especially thankful to escape the banal troubles of Monksford and live a life less ordinary or, as his Aunt had once said, "experience more than mundanity." Despite being only thirty-two, Morgan had seen more of the world than most people and even been to places only visited by a few explorers, researchers and wanderers. Since leaving for university at the age of eighteen, he'd not lived in Monksford for more than a month or so at a time and his stays had been less and less frequent up until shortly after he turned twenty-seven when, after an uncharacteristically long stay in the village of his youth, he suddenly left for central Africa.

Morgan's thoughts drifted between Eliza's notes, his guilt at being away from her for so long and a haunting uncertainty over what to do next. He knew his Aunt had been ill but nothing in the house suggested she had been feeling close to death. There were no letters, no sorting of her affairs – other than Mrs Cartwright's tidying. From her painstaking research it was clear her mind had remained as adept and insightful as ever, although her notes had increasingly referenced source texts he could not find and some notes made little sense. Some were simply labelled 'AA' whilst others were just the letters TNP followed by strings of numbers. Perhaps she had suffered after all, Morgan pondered, the sense of urgency to her notes frequently giving him cause for concern.

Morgan concluded that there was only one place he could find a solution to the cloud of questions in his head: the village pub. The Devil's Due had been built as a coaching house in the

1700s and nobody was sure where the name had come from. Morgan had been a regular visitor from the age of fifteen until he left for university and even after that would frequent it often on his returns to Monksford.

As he walked across the village he alternated between reminiscing about good times in the pub and wondering how much it had changed in the five years since his last visit. It was only when he was at the entrance to the short gravel track that led to the pub colloquially known as The Devil's, and heard the music that he realised it was Friday night and that the place would be far busier than he had anticipated.

Undeterred, he continued down the track, through the large garden and into the main bar. The old oak beams forced him to duck as he entered the hot and crowded room. He looked around, expecting things to be different, but other than a slightly different shade of brown on the walls and one new beer on pump, nothing had changed. A band were playing in the barn, causing every conversation in the bar to be shouted – it was loud and uncomfortable with a layer of cigarette smoke hanging beneath the low ceiling. The familiar sights, smells and sounds filled Morgan with warmth. He ordered an ale that was slightly tepid and returned to the garden. It was a pleasant summer night and most benches were occupied, but one, beneath the branches of a mighty ash tree, was vacant and Morgan sat there quietly, facing the front of the pub, watching people drift in and out as he nursed his pint.

It was towards the end of his first drink that a simple idea occurred to him, a notion so obvious that he was almost annoyed with himself for not having thought of it before. He resolved to contact his aunt's former colleagues at the various universities she had worked at, to find out if she'd spoken to them or if they knew anything about the missing sources mentioned in her notes. He would find Liza's address book over the weekend and start making telephone calls on Monday morning.

Morgan was enjoying the atmosphere outside the pub; the cool and still summer night, the muffled sounds of the band and the buzz of conversation and merry laughter. At one point, he thought he heard a nightjar's call cut across the revelry. He bought himself another drink and returned to his bench beneath the ancient ash. His thoughts drifted between two periods of Monksford's history, the medieval events his aunt had been researching and his own youth. Saxon monks waded across the same river he had fished in as a child; supporters of the King hid from Roundheads in the same forest trees he once climbed. The places we go, Morgan pondered, are a bridge between the past and the present, both personally and in the grand arc of history.

The music died as the band took a break and a small cluster of women emerged from the side door of the barn and into the garden. As they meandered between tables, one of them laughed gaily and the familiarity of the sound caused Morgan to snap out of his daydreams. He saw her only a second or two before she saw him. In that time, the dam holding back his former life burst as her brown hair swept across her shoulders and a thousand memories flooded to the forefront of his mind. She'd been his oldest friend, his closest confidant, the sister he'd never had. Her name had been etched on his heart since the age of ten: Shirley.

It had been five years since he'd last seen her face, yet that time melted in an instant as she saw him across the garden and smiled. 'Morgan!' she yelled, breaking away from the pack and hastily making her way across the garden to the bench beneath the old ash tree, 'You're back!' She sat beside him and hugged him. Morgan smiled as he returned her embrace.

'Yeah,' he replied, breaking the hug, 'I've been back just over a week, I'd have called but –.'

'It's okay. You've had a lot to deal with. I'm sorry about your aunt.' She responded, adjusting her dress slightly.

'Thank you.' Morgan paused, there was so much he could have said in that moment. Part of him wanted to reminisce about the past, another part wanted to express his anguish at missing his aunt's funeral, still another wanted to talk about her book. None of it seemed appropriate, with the sound of laughter and conversation drifting across the lawn and Shirley's friends' occasional glances in their direction. Instead, he asked a simple question, the most important question you can ever ask a dear friend: 'How are you?'

Shirley smiled, tucking a lock of her long brown hair behind her ear, 'I'm doing good. Been up and down but I'm doing admin for a charity in Newton now. I like it.'

Before he could press for more details, one of Shirley's friends came over. She smiled at Shirley but gave Morgan a cold look.

'Shelly, look who's back?'

'I saw,' she replied.

'Nice to see you,' Morgan interjected, with a smile.

'Hm. You too,' Shelly responded sourly before turning back to Shirley, 'The band is about to start, they're going to play a song for Emily.'

'I'll be there in a minute.'

Shelly turned and walked back to the group. 'She's always hated me,' Morgan commented.

A tense silence risked descending upon the pair but Shirley swatted it away with a joke. 'Probably still

bitter about when you told Benji Smith that she like-liked him.'
They both laughed.
'You should go back to your friends. They'll be singing Emily's song in a minute.'
'I haven't seen you in five years. I want to talk to you.' Shirley insisted, a little hurt showing on her face.
'I should go soon anyway. What are you doing tomorrow?'
Shirley chuckled, 'Recovering from tonight I expect. I'm already quite drunk.'
'Well, why don't you come over for a cuppa, we can talk properly. I'm at my Aunt's house.'
'Sounds good,' Shirley replied, standing up and brushing the front of her dress with her hands.
'See you tomorrow.'
Shirley hugged Morgan again before leaving and said seriously, 'You won't disappear again?'
'No, no I'm not going anywhere.'
Morgan watched his oldest friend walk across the garden and, finishing the last of his beer, caught Shelly glaring at him icily as the group made their way inside.

Three:

Morgan spent Saturday morning attempting to keep himself busy despite his excitement and trepidation at seeing Shirley again. He had no idea if and when Shirley would arrive and the minutes dawdled by while Morgan tried to hurry them along by keeping his mind on other matters. He attempted to sort through more of his aunt's possessions, decode her research notes and tidy the cottage, but whatever he did his mind quickly wandered away.

On his first day of a new school, just after first moving to Monksford, when he hadn't known anyone; he had just been a sad little boy stood on the edge of the playground until one brave girl bounced over to him and asked if he knew how to use a skipping rope. He didn't but she taught him. They were inseparable after that, best friends and partners in crime, taking on adolescence as a team. Boyfriends and girlfriends came and went; friendships around them crumbled and flourished and crumbled again but always their little coalition remained.

The long summers of their youth were spent in the great outdoors, just them and their little gang of friends. Building dens and catching frogs gave way to building bonfires and stealing beers.

The stars were their playground, laying on the grass dreaming of all the things to come. A few nights before Morgan left for university, when they were camped out in a meadow with friends for an impromptu farewell gathering, Shirley, who had recently broken up with her boyfriend, took him by the hand and led him into the woods. She kissed him in a grassy clearing and they laid down together amongst the wildflowers. Fuelled by cheap vodka, heartbreak and a love that runs deeper than a river, they fumbled their way into each other's arms.

Their tryst was short lived. After only a few months of his course, she made the long journey to visit him and they lay side by side on his small bed in his tiny room and mutually decided that being more than friends was more than they could handle. They did not suffer for it, if anything their friendship became stronger than ever. Morgan threw himself into academia and Shirley focussed on her career. On his trips home they would still laugh and cut capers across the countryside, whiling away many hours in each other's company. She would visit him too and he would show her the city and introduce her to his new friends. As they followed their own paths, they remained a constant pillar of support for each other, both a beacon in the dark times and the greatest celebrants of each other's successes.

In time Shirley would fall for a friend of a friend, a law student named Kenneth. Morgan, however, would have few romantic entanglements, so consumed as he was by his pursuit of his PhD and his career. He'd had a brief romance with a publisher from the firm that produced his book, though it fell apart soon after he brought her to Monksford for the first time. It was not long after that minor heartbreak that he was invited on an expedition to central Africa and, with no real reason to stay, he left.

Eventually, Morgan gave up with trying to distract himself indoors and, after a light lunch, sat in the garden with a cup of tea and a book his aunt had been reading about witch trials in Britain. He stopped only to replace his empty teacup with a cold drink and to watch a pair of swallows fly past. At just after two o'clock he heard the unmistakable sound of the front gate creek open and shut and took himself around the front to find Shirley on the doorstep.

'Doors open,' he said from behind her.
She jumped, surprised by his angle of approach.
'You sod!' she declared.
'I was round the back and heard you coming.' He said as they hugged fondly. 'Shall I put the kettle on?' Morgan asked.
'It's too hot to drink tea. I've got the kayaks and the van, let's go down the river.'

Morgan turned and saw the yellow Volkswagen camper parked in the road with two grey-green kayaks tied to the roof-rack. 'Wow. You've still got it.' The van had belonged to Shirley's parents, who had been hippies until her dad had inherited the family business and been forced to settle down. It had been passed on to her and Morgan had many fond memories of road trips and adventures in the old 'love wagon'.

    Morgan changed into more suitable clothes and hopped into the van. It had been well looked after over the years and ran well in spite of its age. 'They don't make them like the used to' had been Shirley's father's motto.

'So, how was Africa?' Shirley asked as they drove towards the river.

Morgan sighed, 'A colossal failure, to be honest. We spent five years going up and down the Congo looking for evidence of some rumoured ancient Bantu city that probably never existed. When I think about all the great explorers and archaeologists I read about as a child, I just wonder if there's anything left to discover.'

'I'm sure that's not true,' Shirley interjected. 'You're only thirty-two, there's still loads of time. You've already done so much, been to Mexico, Egypt, Turkey and across Central Africa, got a book published. You should be proud.'

'You're right, I'm just being morose. I worry I wasted half a decade on that expedition and, you know, because of that I didn't get to say goodbye to my aunt – who basically raised me.'

Shirley turned the van down a small track and parked in a layby close to the river. 'That's not your fault,' she explained, 'You were half a world away in the middle of the jungle, or whatever. You came as soon as you could.'

'I wish I'd tried harder to go back to the city, to check in with everyone more often.'

'You can't beat yourself up,' Shirley insisted, climbing out the van, 'Your aunt would have understood. She was proud of you and pleased you were following your dreams. Now, come on, give me a hand with these kayaks.'

Shirley didn't need much help, she had always been strong, but Morgan carried one boat and some gear down to the river anyway and helped set the kayaks up. Shirley tied back her long hair before helping a struggling Morgan with the spray deck. She laughed warmly as he swished the rubber as if it were a skirt, the same joke he had pulled on every prior kayaking trip.

They launched the boats and paddled downstream, away from Monksford. They chatted and joked along the way, falling silent from time to time to soak in the sunshine and the beauty of the scenery around them. Shirley's toned physique gave her a significant advantage over the wiry Morgan, but she regularly stopped to wait for the less experienced boater.

'I heard you and Ken broke up.' Morgan remarked as they passed into a shaded length of river, where the tops of the tall trees lining both banks met in the middle.

'That was ages ago. Who told you?'

'Mrs Cartwright. She tried to fill me in on all the village news.'

'She does love to gossip,' Shirley chuckled, 'It's okay, we didn't have much in common; he just wanted an old-fashioned housewife and that's not me. Plus, he really hated doing anything like this.'

Morgan knew Shirley well enough to sense that she had no desire to discuss the details, so gave her the opportunity to change the subject as he watched a dragonfly flit amongst the sunbeams. 'How could anyone hate this? This is perfect.'

Shirley smiled, 'Better than the Congo?'

'Much better. No crocodiles.'

They laughed and continued their way downstream. The river widened gradually, as it twisted across the countryside, through woodland and alongside meadows. They passed under an old stone bridge, just high enough for them to navigate, where a young child waved at them enthusiastically from the back of a stationary car.

Shortly after passing a derelict stone barn, they arrived at a natural river island with grass banks and a pair of willow trees. They pulled the kayaks ashore and rested in the shade. The air was still and full of the gentle chirping of birds above them.

'I remember this place, we used to come here all the time.'

'It's a lovely spot,' Shirley replied, as she lay back in the grass.

'I've missed this,' said Morgan, as he lay beside her. 'What will you do now your back? Will you stay in Monksford long?'

'I don't know. Aunt 'Liza was writing a book; I'd like to finish it for her.'

'What was it about?' enquired Shirley, turning on her side to face him.

'It was all about the history of Monksford. Some interesting things happened here.'

'Yeah,' Shirley replied drily.

'No really, it's in the Doomsday book and there were witch trials here. In the 13th Century a meteorite crashed into the hills just outside the village, caused quite a stir.'

'A meteorite? Like the one a couple of years ago?'

'What do you mean a couple of years ago?' replied Morgan, confused.

'Two Summers ago, a meteor crashed near Monksford. Didn't you hear?'

'No, I didn't know anything about it.'

'You mean Mrs Cartwright told you about me and Ken breaking up but didn't think to mention a space rock nearly hitting the village?'

'She also told me about all about Mrs. Johnson's cat.'

Shirley shook her head and laughed.

'Are you telling me another meteorite crashed near Monksford?' asked Morgan.

'I didn't know about the first one, but yeah. It was national news, the village was swarming with scientists, journalists and crazy folk who look for little green men. They took away some of it for research but most of it is still up there. I'll take you up tomorrow if you like.'

'Yes please. I'd love to see it.'

'My mum still has all the newspaper cuttings, as well, if you want to have a look.'

Morgan laughed, 'We always used to say that nothing exciting ever happens in Monksford. But what are the chances? Two meteorites crashing next to the same village? Even if it is seven hundred years apart, it's quite a story.'

'Maybe that's why your aunt was writing about Monksford, wanted people to know it had happened before.'

'Maybe. Either way, I'd love to go and see it and have a look at the articles.'

Shirley spent the journey back upstream telling Morgan everything she remembered about the meteorite: 'I was in Newton, some of us had gone for a meal after work for somebody's birthday. It was only just starting to get dark and I was walking across the car park when I saw it streak across the sky. There had been loads of little ones, shooting stars, for weeks, but this was much bigger and orange. Left a sort of trail behind it – apparently it was from some of it vaporising in the atmosphere. It was beautiful but I didn't think anything more of it. There was no crashing sound or flash of light – not in Newton anyway. A couple of fire engines and police cars went past me while I was driving back but I didn't make the connection.

'When I got home, everyone in our street was outside talking about it, I was living with Mum and Dad at the time. Dad had been putting the bins out and seen it shoot past, much lower by then. Seconds later, he said, there was a distant crashing sound. It came down in the woods on top of Dunmoor Hill. They were fighting fires all night; fire crews came from miles away to help, there were helicopters everywhere. Amazingly no one was hurt.

'The police cordoned off the area for weeks – that's when all the scientists and journalists were coming and going. I think they wanted to keep the weirdos away as well as making sure it was safe. It left a trail of fragments all across the fields and woods between here and town, everyone was out looking for them the next day, trying to get their hands on their own space rock. The only injuries were caused by people trying to pick up rocks that were still hot.

'It was big news. All the shops and pubs in the area were trying to cash in. One guy was arrested for selling gravel that he said was from the rock but wasn't. In the end they said it was safe and lifted the cordon. We still get people come to the area to see it but mostly everything is back to normal now. I'm surprised you could be back in Monksford for a week and a half, or whatever, and not hear about it though – or have you just been keeping to yourself all the time?'

'Mostly,' Morgan replied, 'You know how it is.'

'I know how you are.' Shirley said with a grin, 'We're nearly back at the van. I'll race you the rest of the way. Loser buys the first round. Three... two... one... go!'

Before Morgan could respond Shirley was tearing through the water ahead of him. He tried to keep up but he had never been as strong as her and hadn't kayaked in years. By the time he breathlessly paddled around the last bend, she had hauled her kayak out of the water and was patting her damp clothes down with a towel.

'Hurry up,' Shirley chuckled, 'Pub closes in seven hours.'

After about an hour in the pub, swapping stories of Monksford with stories of the Congo basin, the two old friends parted. Shirley offered Morgan a lift but he chose to walk home, reflecting on the day's revelations. He wondered why his aunt, in spite of her age, had been so determined to write a book about Monksford and if the meteorite incident really had inspired her, as Shirley had speculated. He thought about the missing sources and hoped that speaking to Aunt 'Liza's contacts would shed some light on the mystery. He asked himself if he knew anyone who could suggest whether there could be a connection between the two meteorite impacts or if it was really just a coincidence. Most of his mind, however, was consumed with the strange mix of feelings he'd had around Shirley throughout the afternoon. At times it felt as if they had never parted, as if their friendship was the same as it had always been. There were moments, however, where he felt as if a chasm existed between them, some great void created by his absence that they could never fully overcome, no matter how they tried.

Four:

As promised, Shirley came over the next morning with the newspaper cuttings. Heavy rain, however, scuppered their plans to hike up to the crater.
'My sister is visiting Mum and Dad with the kids, so I should probably go over there anyway.' She explained, sheltering just inside the front door.
'Are you sure you can't stay for a cuppa?'
'Not really, they're expecting me back for lunch. I told them I was just popping out to drop these off.' She handed Morgan a folder, wrapped in a shopping bag, 'To be honest, I just wanted ten minutes away from those screaming kids. Perhaps we can go up to the crater one evening in the week.'
'That sounds good, let me know.' Morgan smiled.
'Will do. I won't hug you because I'm soaked – see you later.'

Morgan watched Shirley run down the pathway and drive away in her van. He took the folder, still wrapped up, into the kitchen and put it on the side while he put the kettle on. He watched the rain run down the kitchen window while the water boiled, made himself a cup of tea and then opened the folder out on the kitchen table. The newspaper cuttings were from a combination of The Newton Post - their local rag, and various national papers that had also covered the story. The Post had clearly taken full advantage of the story and covered it in immense detail for many months. The paper speculated wildly, frequently printed retractions of the same speculations and appeared to have interviewed almost the entire village, as well as many visitors, from notable scientists to roving conspiracy theorists.

Despite the sheer volume of speculation about the meteorite, Morgan was quickly able to fill many of the holes in Shirley's story with solid facts. A meteorite weighing just under three metric tonnes and composed of iron, nickel and small amounts of other substances had crashed into the woods on top of Dunmoor Hill on the 20th of June, with small fragments spread across the countryside between Newton and Monksford. It started several fires in the woods, which had proved incredibly difficult to extinguish due to the preceding dry weather. The area around the meteorite was cordoned off while scientists studied the rock to ensure it was not radioactive and presented no other dangers. It then received many visitors, much to the annoyance of the landowner, who threatened to have it removed but eventually relented and permitted visitors. Over the following months a mixture of locals and UFO hunters claimed to see extra-terrestrial visitors in and around the village, but the photos presented were quickly proven to be fakes and suggestions that the meteorite was an alien vessel were easily debunked. There was no mention in any of the articles about the previous meteorite impact, in the thirteenth century. Aunt Liza, it appeared, had seemed content to keep that information to herself, at least for the time being.

The final article in the folder, dated six months after the impact, provided an unexpected revelation to Morgan as he read it. It detailed the findings of the studies into the meteorite samples removed by scientists and taken to university laboratories across the country:

"Scientists studying the meteorite which crashed into woodland close to Monksford earlier this year have concluded that it may have originated from the Kuiper Belt, a disc of rock and dust at the edge of the Solar System. Despite being originally classified as a 'pallasite', one of the rarest types of meteorite, with initial findings suggesting it was a stray asteroid from the belt between Mars and Jupiter, trace amounts of methane and ammonia have suggested a more unusual origin.

"The meteorite impact, first reported by TNP, has been the subject of much scientific interest and this study, conducted by experts at the University of Cambridge, looks set to finally answer the question of what the rock is made of and where it came from."

Morgan stopped reading and jumped out of his chair, fetching his aunt's notes from the other room. TNP had been the name of one of his aunt's sources that Morgan had been unable to identify and now he knew what it was: *The Newton Post*. The string of numbers had been dates and page numbers. With the exception of five references, all of the TNP sources were articles included in Shirley's mum's folder.

By spending the afternoon cross-referencing the articles with his aunt's notes and other source texts, Morgan was able to confirm Shirley's theory that Aunt 'Liza had taken an interest in the meteorite. There was also some suggestion that his aunt had believed there to be a connection between the 13th Century meteorite and the most recent impact, though he had little idea what that connection was. Morgan decided to take a walk, despite the rain, and go over some of the facts in his head, hoping for a little more clarity.

He donned a large waterproof coat and some walking boots, pulling his hood over his head as he left the cottage. The sound of the raindrops gently striking the material was comforting and soon Morgan was pacing through Prince's Wood, close to the river. He walked as though in a daze, drifting off the main path and down a side track that led towards a stream. As the woods grew heavy around him the musky smell of fresh rain and pine slowly became malodorous and dank. A chill ran down his spine as the dense branches eclipsed the overcast sky. He didn't know this path but it felt familiar. Despite an increasingly oppressive atmosphere Morgan continued down towards the stream, trying to ignore the strange movements of the trees around him. Cold, damp and filled with a haunting melancholy, Morgan stopped and stared at the vista before him. A dead oak tree, stood in a small clearing by the putrid stream, its bare branches reaching out menacingly. Suddenly, he remembered being here before, deep in the many-fabled woods.

They'd been about twelve or thirteen; Morgan, Shirley and a few others, playing in the woods late one summer afternoon; riding bikes and building dens. Morgan, Shirley and a boy named Graham, someone's little brother inflicted on the group by an exasperated mother, were looking for big branches and had stumbled upon the forsaken clearing with the rotting tree at its heart, disturbing a huge flock of crows. On the very spot where he now stood, the three of them had been frozen, eyes transfixed by the horror before them. Shirley had reacted fastest, covering Graham's eyes and turning him away. From one mighty branch of the old oak hung a rope and from that rope hung the decaying corpse of a young woman. The stench had been overwhelming, it was the first time any of them had seen a body and the sight was harrowing. Shirley shook Morgan's arm and shouted at him. The three children turned and ran back towards the others. They'd all ridden their bikes back to the village as fast as they could and called the police from the nearest house.

The sounds of a dog barking broke Morgan from his daze. The rain had eased and the branches of the skeletal oak tree were empty. The malaise that had momentarily held him had been nothing more than the spectre of a dark memory he had buried deep in the furthest recesses of his mind. As he made his way back towards the main path, he was relieved to find that the ghostly atmosphere he had imagined had vanished – nothing more than his own psyche warning him away from the foul clearing and the ill-forged memories that inhabited it.

As he reached the top of the track, a black dog bounded into view, barking cheerfully, followed by the less energetic but no-less cheerful figure of old Mr Cartwright. "Ello Young'un!' He said with a wink and a smile, 'What you doing out here in the rain?'

'Hello Mr Cartwright. Just clearing my head a little.' Morgan replied.

'How many times do I have to tell you? Call me Tom. Otherwise, I'm going to start calling you Dr Black.'

'Yes mist-. Yes Tom.' Morgan chuckled, 'Walking Bruce?'

'Oh yes. On my way up to The Devil's, thought I'd get a couple of drinks in before the missus gets back from evensong. Fancy a pint?'

'Sounds like a good idea.' Morgan said, falling into step alongside the old gentleman.

'I hear you're writing a book about Monksford.'

'Who told you that?'

'What's her name? Brenda, your mate Shirley's mum, was telling Cathy after church this morning. 'Parrently you were after some newspaper cuttings.'

'Word gets round fast. Yeah, Aunt 'Liza was working on something, I want to finish it off for her.'

'Well, if there's anything I can help with,' offered Tom as they hopped over the style opposite the pub garden, 'I've been living in the village all my life.'

'There is one thing,' Morgan ventured, 'Though it isn't to do with the book. Do you remember when I was a child, some friends and I found a body in the woods?'

'Yeah, I remember. Unpleasant business that.'

'That's what I was going to ask. I don't remember it very well and was wondering if they ever found out who she was.'

'She was a tourist, Canadian I think, decided to spend the night in the woods for some reason. Poor thing. There's some horrible place in those woods, all sorts of stories.'
'Yeah, I remember.'

Tom led Morgan into the pub and sat in his usual spot at the bar. The place was almost deserted, in stark contrast to Friday night, and the hefty landlord was sat at the bar lazily flicking through a newspaper.
'Afternoon Tom,' he said, rising slowly and making his way back behind the bar, 'Usual?'
'Yes, please Kevin, and one for Morgan. You remember Eliza Black's nephew, don't you?'
'Ah yes, the one who went to Africa. What'll it be, son?'
'Pint of bitter, please,' Morgan requested, 'Thanks Tom.'
Tom nodded and engaged Kevin in some small talk about the sudden rain, while he poured the drinks. As the landlord handed his pint over, Morgan asked him if he knew the story behind the pub's name.
'It's funny you should say that,' the publican explained, 'Your Aunt was in 'ere, no more than a couple of months back, an' told me 'bout it.'
'Aunt 'Liza was in here?' Morgan responded, almost choking on his beer, much to Tom's amusement.

'Historical event that,' the old man quipped, 'Ought to put it in your book.'

'Aye, she comes in with some foreign gent.' Kevin replied, '"Pparently, he was some expert in ghosts or summit, wanted to see this place on account of it bein' 'aunted.'

'Haunted? This place isn't haunted.' Morgan said looking around him.

'Strange place is Monksford,' Tom interjected over the rim of his glass, 'Them woods, this place and the meteorites. Who knows what's possible?'

The archaeologist shook his head, 'I don't believe in ghosts, ghouls and little green men.'

'Neither did I,' Kevin replied, 'But since takin' over this place, I'm not so sure. Let me tell you, every night I go round checking no glasses have been left out, saves a job in the mornin' see. Every night I clear the bar down, lock up and go upstairs, but every mornin' there's four glasses left out, little bit of ale in the bottom of each one. No one's been in or out but every morning they're there, as if four blokes have popped in for a quick pint and dashed off, in the middle of the night, except the place is all locked up and there's no way in or out.'

Tom looked at Morgan expectantly, 'Well?' He asked.

'I don't know, I'm just sceptical about these things.'

'Well, this friend of your aunt, foreign chap,' Kevin continued, 'He says he knows the place is haunted, can feel the ghostly presence 'ere. Learned man too, some professor, carrying a big old book with him.'

'Owning a big book doesn't make you an expert. Did you catch his name?'

'Some foreign name, I don't know.'

'Strange, I wonder who he was. Anyway, what about the pub's name? What did my aunt say about that?'

'It's an old story, she said, from long before there was a pub here. Some local lord, had one son and one daughter and his son goes off to fight in a war. The lord is really worried about it because if his son is killed then there's no one to inherit his lands and titles. He's walking across his land one day, worrying about it and a devil comes to him.'

'A devil? You mean the devil?'

'No, not the actual devil, like one of his servants.'

'I see, sorry, carry on.'

'The lord makes a deal with this devil. The devil says that he'll protect his son and that one day, when his son has returned, he'll come back and ask for something in return. The lord is so desperate that he accepts the devil's offer.'

'I can see where this is going,' Tom quips.

'Right. Then one day the son comes back and the lord is delighted. The next night the devil comes to him and tells him what he wants in return, the daughter, who is just about to come of age. The

lord refuses to give her to him and the next day both the son and daughter come over sick. Within a week both are dead because the devil, as the saying goes, always gets his due.'
'What happened to the lord?' Morgan enquired.
'He went mad with grief. Went into the woods and hung himself on some old oak tree.'

Five:

The rain showers of Sunday continued well into the following day. Morgan spent most of the next day on a chair in the hallway, armed with a notepad and his aunt's address book, telephoning some of Eliza's former colleagues. Although he had several very pleasant conversations, with everyone having incredibly kind words to say about his aunt, there was little information of practical use. Some former colleagues and contacts told Morgan they had spoken to her since she had begun working on the book, some had recommended particular pieces of literature to her, but none could solve the riddle of the 'AA' references in Eliza's notebook. He also asked if any knew the foreign gentleman who had visited only a few months ago, but without a name or more details none were able to help. Morgan thanked each one in turn before sighing heavily and making the next phone call.

    Eventually, Morgan abandoned the address book and attempted to make contact with his own former professor, who had been a colleague of Eliza's many years previously. Now that he was retired, it took some effort to persuade the university to relinquish his contact details. However, once he explained who he was and what he wanted, they relented. The telephone rang for a long time before the professor answered.

'Hello, James Lambert speaking.'

'Professor. It's Morgan Black.'

'Oh, hello! Good to hear from you,' the professor responded, his privileged upbringing instantly clear from his manner of speaking, 'Very sorry about your aunt. We came to the funeral, such a shame you weren't able to, terrible business.'

'They delayed it as long as they could but sadly no one was able to get in contact with me until it was too late, what with the political situation where I was.'

'Civil war didn't give you any trouble other than that? I was quite worried.'

'Not at all, we were a long way from the fighting – we just couldn't get back to the city for a few months.'

'And how was the expedition?' enquired the professor.

'A disaster, to be quite frank. Besides the issues caused by the conflict we weren't able to find any evidence of a Bantu city along the Congo. The evidence that had been presented in the past turned out to be either false or had disappeared entirely.'

'A shame, but it happens to us all. I remember one of my first digs was an entire spring, with your aunt as it happens, on Crete. I had dreams of uncovering

Ancient Greek ruins, a temple or a palace perhaps. Instead, all we found was medieval pottery, tonnes and tonnes of it.'

'At least you found something.' Morgan commented.

'That is exactly what your aunt said – ever the optimist. What are you doing now that you're back? I still hold some sway at the university, I'm sure I could persuade them to offer you a position. If you want to go back into the field, Doctor Whelan is planning an expedition to Iraq, I'm sure she'd love to have you on board.'

'Thank you, professor, but I'm currently trying to finish a book I believe my aunt was working on about the history of Monksford. I'm wondering, did she speak to you about it?'

'Not really my field of expertise, my boy. The last time we spoke was about six months ago and it was just a catch up, the only thing she asked me, besides if I'm enjoying retirement and how the boys are, was if I'd heard anything from your expedition.'

'Right, okay,' replied Morgan despondently.

'What's the matter?'

'Well, it's Aunt 'Liza's research. The earlier stuff I can make a lot of sense out of, it's all the usual bits and pieces: Doomsday Book, Norman church, some interesting documents about witch trials, a few local legends and some stuff about the Civil War.'

'Right? I'm with you so far.'
'Then it starts to get a little bit vague, I'm afraid. She had a visitor a few months ago, a foreign gentleman, by all accounts. I don't know his name. She seems to have shown him around the village, so perhaps she discussed things with him. You don't know who he could be, by any chance?'
'I'm afraid not,' the professor replied, 'foreign, did you say?'
'Yes, though I don't know where he was from. Not to worry.' Morgan paused before continuing, 'She seems to have been looking quite intensely into the meteorite that crashed nearby a couple of years ago, she'd read lots of newspaper reports and a couple of academic papers. Then she found out, from an old manuscript kept in a nearby abbey, that there'd been another meteor in the thirteenth century. This clearly piqued her interest.'
'Understandably, two meteorite impacts near the same village does sound unusual,' interjected the professor.
'After that it gets much harder to decode. Her notes are less comprehensive and seem to have been written hastily. She starts referencing something she calls AA a lot, it seemed very important. I've checked all her books, there's no texts or writers that fit the initials AA and make sense. It seems like it was her link between the two meteorites.'

'Interesting,' the professor mused, 'have you considered that the link might not be historical?'
'What do you mean?'
'Well, you're talking about the link between two astronomical events. Perhaps you need to talk to an astronomer.'
'Of course!' Morgan declared, 'Thank you professor, I'll do just that.'

It wasn't until the next morning that Morgan was able to get in contact with someone from the astronomy department of his old university, one Doctor Singh.
'Let me just check I understand,' Doctor Singh began, in response to Morgan's explanation, 'There are two meteorites, seven hundred years apart that impacted close to each other and you're wondering if there could be a connection?'
'That's right. The most recent one was a pallasite,' Morgan said glancing at his notes, 'possibly from the Kuiper belt. I don't know any details about the older one.'
'To be honest, it's unlikely there's a real connection. Europe does receive an unusually high number of meteorite-falls compared to other continents, especially given its size. Even so, two meteorites falling so close to each other is a remarkable coincidence but probably just a coincidence. Without a sample of the older

meteorite, it's impossible to say if they are similar in any way but pallasites are rare so it is unlikely that they are both in that class. Have you considered that the earlier meteorite is just a myth? Without any physical evidence, that could be one conclusion.'

'It's possible,' replied Morgan, 'But my Aunt got her information from records in a nearby abbey that are generally considered reliable, though I have found no mention of it elsewhere and I have no idea what became of the rock itself.'

'Two meteorites impacting so close to each other would be remarkable, if it could be proven. If those two meteorites turned out to be similar in some way, that would be even more remarkable but we would probably still call it a coincidence. I'm sorry but I don't think there is a connection.'

'Thank you for your time. One other thing, I know that you are busy but do the initials AA mean anything to you. It appears to be a source text my aunt was referencing.'

'AA is the ionisation constant but I can't think of any physicists or other experts with those initials that relate to this matter. I'm sorry.'

Morgan was not discouraged. He firmly believed that his aunt had uncovered something of value and was determined to complete her work. To that end, after lunch, he caught a bus to Newton in order to visit the offices of The Newton Post, in hope of finding the five articles his aunt had referenced that were not in Shirley's mum's folder.

He arrived a little after two and was welcomed by a receptionist with whom he had earlier conversed on the telephone. He had already impressed his academic credentials on her, in the hope of overcoming any reluctance towards his visit. She was, however, entirely co-operative, providing him with a coffee and cheerfully showing him the newspaper's impressive repository of local happenings dating back almost fifty years. Morgan was adept at perusing an archive such as this, a skill he had acquired during his post-graduate years, and quickly found the articles that concerned him. Disappointingly, Morgan was unable to see a connection with these articles and his aunt's research around either the meteorite or the wider history of Monksford. Three of the pieces were front page articles concerned a missing teenager, who disappeared almost exactly a year before – around the time Morgan believed his aunt to have begun her research. Another was a short article and accompanying picture about a rabid fox and the final one was an interview with a prominent America UFO hunter and consisted almost entirely of pseudo-scientific nonsense.

With the rain now clear, Morgan left the newspaper offices and sat on a bench by the canal idly flicking through his notepad and watching a narrowboat float by, brooding on another dead end in his research. After a short time, he walked back through town to the deserted cemetery, where he stood beside his aunt's grave, to further ponder the situation. 'Here lieth,' he read aloud, 'Eliza Maria Black. Archaeologist and historian. "Undying in eternity lies, until death itself may die".' The strange choice of quote made Morgan furrow his eyebrows in puzzlement, 'Undying in eternity lies, until death itself may die.' He repeated, 'Where is that from?'

Suddenly, he felt a presence behind him and a hand upon his shoulder. Morgan jumped forward and turned around, treading clumsily on the flowers he had placed on top of the grave.
'Shirley? You scared me!'
'Sorry,' she chuckled, 'I really didn't mean to. I was coming out of the office over the road and saw you coming in, thought I'd offer you a lift back to Monksford.'
'That'd be nice thanks,' he said, stepping back off of the grave.
'Are you okay?' she said, glancing between Morgan and the wounded flowers.
'Yeah. I was just,' Morgan paused, 'Do you know where this epitaph is from?'
Shirley examined the quote, 'I've never heard it before. It's a bit odd, isn't it?'
'That's what I thought.'

'Maybe it just means that no one really dies. That death isn't the end.'
'I think so. It just seems very strange.' Morgan remarked.
Shirley put her arm round Morgan and rested her head on his shoulder, 'Maybe it meant something to your aunt.'
'Maybe.'

Shirley gave Morgan a lift back to the cottage and arranged to pick him up an hour later so they could go up Dunmoor Hill to see the meteorite that evening. Morgan wasn't quite ready when Shirley came back for him, so she waited in the kitchen, absentmindedly flicking through the chaotic assortment of books, notepads and pieces of paper spread across the table. She picked up a large black notebook and began leafing through it. The dainty handwriting was unfamiliar to her – presumably Eliza's – and mostly consisted of initials, numbers and short descriptions with arrows connecting them. Shirley found it all to be completely meaningless and was astounded Morgan had managed to make as much sense out of these notes as he had. The latter half of the book was blank and Shirley casually fanned through the pages, causing a photograph to fall from and land, face up, on the table. Shirley put down the book and carefully picked up the photo. It was a picture of Eliza Back and an old man she didn't recognise, taken in the grounds of Monksford's Norman church. One wall of the church stood behind them, with a small side door standing open. The date written on the back showed the photo to be only a few months old and was accompanied by a short description, written in scratchy handwriting, "With Doctor Eliza Black, Monksford, examining local secrets."

Morgan called out as he came down the stairs, 'Sorry about that, I'm ready now. Where are you?'
'In here,' Shirley replied as Morgan entered the room, 'Have you seen this?'
Morgan put down his small rucksack, took the photograph from Shirley's outstretched hand and examined both sides.
'Who is it?' Shirley asked.
'I don't know. Kevin at The Devil's said Aunt 'Liza was in there with a foreign gentleman a few months ago. Maybe this was him.'
'What do you think "examining local secrets" means?' Shirley asked, pointing at the note on the back of the photograph.
'I don't know, apparently he was looking for ghost stories. Where is this taken?' Morgan replied, furrowing his eyebrows.
'That's the back of St James' church.'

'I'll have to go and have a look tomorrow. Right, shall we go?' Morgan said, depositing the photograph in his bag.

Shirley drove the old camper van to The Devil's Due and parked in the carpark around the side of the pub. Morgan popped inside to check with Kevin if the man in the photograph was the same man who had visited the pub with Aunt 'Liza. Kevin confirmed Morgan's theory but when pressed could remember no more details about the conversation. Morgan thanked Kevin and told him that it was very helpful, which was only a slight exaggeration, before returning to the car park.

'Are you coming down again on Friday?' Shirley enquired as she hopped over the style.

'I don't know. What's happening?'

'Just a band, I think.'

'Maybe,' replied Morgan as he followed behind her, 'I'll see how I feel.'

The two old friends walked through Prince's Woods, across a footbridge and along the narrow footpath that separated two farmers' fields. The evening sun was warm and the yellow, gold and green fields around them were alive with a multitude of birds. They laughed and joked as they ambled across the countryside. Morgan updated Shirley on the details of his research and Shirley told Morgan every detail she could remember about the meteorite. They reminded each other of different local legends and chuckled together while reminiscing about growing up together in Monksford. The mood was light as the two walked beside one another and Morgan felt happier than he had in many years.

'Did you meet anyone in Africa?' Shirley asked casually, as they hopped over a style and onto the wooded footpath that snaked its way up Dunmoor Hill.

'Of course, there were huge teams working on the digs, both from here and universities in Kinshasa and Brazzaville.'

Shirley rolled her eyes, 'No, I mean did you meet any women? Romantically?'

'Oh,' replied Morgan, genuinely surprised, 'No. There was nothing like that.'

'Nothing at all?'

'I went out for dinner a couple of times with a woman who worked at the university in Kinshasa but it didn't go anywhere.'

'What was her name?'

'Nneka,' Morgan answered, 'She was nice.'

'What happened?' Shirley persisted.

'Nothing. We went out for dinner a few times and that was it.'

'No, I mean, why didn't it go further?'

Morgan stopped walking and crouched down to tie up a shoelace that had come loose, 'We agreed not to. I was going to be leaving Kinshasa soon. I promised to write to her when I got back to England – which I will.' Morgan stood up and took the opportunity to change the subject, 'Are we close?'

'A little further,' Shirley replied as they began walking again, 'You can start to see where some of the fires were.'

Sure enough, as they rounded the next bend, they started to witness occasional bare patches amongst the woods accompanied by the skeletal husks of burnt trees. 'This is strange,' Morgan commented, 'I thought it would be one big fire but it looks as if some individual trees just burnt up and not the ones around them.'

Shirley shrugged and they wandered further up the long path.

The lush green forest around them suddenly gave way to a huge and terrifying hellscape. The pink evening sky cast an eerie glow on the scorched remains of hundreds of toppled and twisted trees, their monochrome limbs bent and broken with bonelike branches contorted or lying mangled on the ground. The mutilated forest made a cold shiver run down Morgan's spine. Even after all this time, the warm breeze blew pieces of ash through the air. Some trees remained standing, their blackened form towering over their fallen brothers, many were dismembered and all were scorched. The forest was strangely silent, as if bird

and beast alike had grown weary of this woodland necropolis. Patches of grass and wildflowers grew in small clumps scattered across the grey earth, a rare splash of colour on an otherwise entirely bleak scene. Morgan bent down to inspect the dusty ground around a patch of bluebells. 'I'm surprised more hasn't grown in this time,' he commented.
'There were lots of mushrooms last year,' Shirley replied, 'Dad was up here picking as many as he could.'
'I think that's quite normal after a fire,' Morgan replied, standing, 'Where's the crater then?'

They walked a short distance along a well-worn path through the detritus and up to a sudden ridge around a large hole in the ground around fifteen meters across and five meters deep. Morgan stood in awe, 'Wow!' he declared, 'That's bigger than I expected.'
Shirley smiled, 'Incredible, isn't it?' and began carefully making her way down the gentle slope and into the crater, slowly at first before breaking into a run close to the bottom. She turned back towards Morgan, 'Come on.'
Morgan gingerly began his descent, after a few steps he crouched down, using his hands to slow himself and delicately worked his way down the slope. Shirley chuckled at him and Morgan threw her a look, 'I'm not breaking my ankle,' he said dryly. It took only half a minute for Morgan to

reach the bottom but Shirley still jested about his slower pace. Morgan grinned as he stood up, dusting his hands off on his trousers, 'See, not a problem.'

Together they walked a few steps to the rock in the centre of the crater, now easily visible. Morgan had already seen numerous photographs but none of them had captured its raw beauty or the strange sense of wonder it inspired. The meteorite was roughly cubical, the size of a dining table, mostly grey in colour with a smooth glassy texture interrupted by numerous gold-coloured fragments. The summer evening's fading light reflected unusually off of its surface, making it appear to glow as if lit by an internal fire.

Captivated by the subtle changes in colour as his shadow passed across it, Morgan reached out and touched its cold, smooth surface. As he ran his hands over it, he came across a series of grooves carved into the rock's surface. He motioned Shirley to crouch beside him, 'Feel this,' he whispered.
'Yes,' she said as he guided her hand into the small gouge, 'I feel it.'
'Something's been carved into it. It's smooth, not too deep – carved with some skill, by the feel of it.' Morgan took off his bag and withdrew a piece of paper and a large crayon. 'Tools of the trade,' he smiled. He placed the paper over the grooves, held it gently in place with one hand and ran the crayon

gently around the inside of the grooves, producing an outline of the carved image.

'It's probably just some graffiti,' Shirley said dismissively as she stood up.

'Whatever it is,' Morgan replied, examining the image, 'It's very strange'. He handed her the paper, 'Have you ever seen anything like that before?'

Shirley stared at the strange symbol etched in red crayon, the outline of a twisted five-pointed star, 'It's familiar,' she said, 'But I'm not sure.'

Morgan furrowed his brow as he took back the paper and placed it carefully in his bag, 'I don't think I've ever seen anything like it before,' he said.

The long shadow inside the crater loomed over them as the sun began to fade. 'We'd best get back before it gets too dark,' Shirley said with a smile, 'Don't want to end up lost in Prince's Woods for the night.'

Six:

The previous night's walk had worn Morgan out and he slept long into the morning, which was very unusual for him. He had enjoyed himself though and promised himself more long walks in future. After a long and dreamless sleep, he finally woke to the sound of the telephone ringing. It took him a long moment to recognise the sound, it was the first time anyone had called since his return to his aunt's cottage, and he made his way down the stairs in his bedclothes to answer. He tried to cover the fatigue in his voice, 'Hello. Morgan Black speaking.'
'Oh, good morning Morgan, I was just about to ring off. How are you?' The cheer in the professor's voice made Morgan feel even more tired.
'I'm well thank you professor and yourself?'
'Yes, my dear boy, I am as good as always.'
'Glad to hear,' replied Morgan before covering the mouthpiece to hide a yawn.
'Now, I must apologise if I've disturbed you but I've been racking my brains since you called me on Monday and in the middle of the night, I had a thought. It's not about AA, I'm afraid, but about that foreign visitor your aunt had.'
'Yes?' Morgan responded.
'Could it be Dr Zelig?'

'Dr Zelig? I'm not sure I know who that is.'

'He's a German antiquities expert. She met him when she was in America, back in the '60s. I know she visited him every time she went over there and he's visited here too.' the professor explained, 'It might not be him, but it is possible.'

'Yes, I think I vaguely remember him coming over when I was a child. Do you know how I can speak to him?'

'He works at Miskatonic University in Massachusetts. I'll give you the number.'

Morgan had already dialled the first three numbers when he realised that the time difference between the UK and America would make it extremely unlikely that anyone would answer. He hung up and quickly calculated that two o'clock would be the earliest he could reasonably expect an answer.

Morgan took himself into the kitchen, drank some coffee, dressed and made his way to St James' church, in the hope of finding the 'local secret' described on the back of the photograph Shirley had found. Using the picture as a reference he was quickly able to find the spot where the photo was taken. He tried the small, wooden door that was open in the picture's background but found it locked so ventured into the old stone structure's main entrance instead.

The church was much like any English village church, a cavernous space with a high ceiling, brightly lit by a vast and colourful stained-glass window that dominated the wall behind the altar. Silhouetted by the window, in the space between a golden lectern in the shape of an eagle, and the wooden pulpit, stood two figures engaged in conversation, Mrs Cartwright and a man in clerical garb, who Morgan assumed was the local vicar. Morgan sat down on a wooden pew and gazed idly at the woollen hassock hanging on the back of the pew in front, while he waited for the conversation to end.

The discussion at the front of the church became animated and Morgan couldn't help but overhear. Mrs Cartwright appeared to be furious about some changes to the flower arranging rota and the vicar was attempting to calmly explain things to her. Eventually Mrs Cartwright stormed off, leaving the vicar looking somewhat relieved at the front of the church. Morgan made his way to the front of the church and introduced himself. 'Don't worry,' he added, 'I'm not here to talk about the flowers.'

The vicar chuckled, 'I'm Adam,' he said, shaking Morgan's hand, 'Pleasure to meet you.' The vicar was a well-groomed and smart looking man with a kind smile who appeared to be on the good side of forty. 'Do you live in the village?' He asked.

'Sort of,' Morgan replied, 'I used to live here and am back sorting out my aunt's affairs.'

'Oh. I'm sorry for your loss.' Adam sat on the edge of the front pew and Morgan took the same position the other side of the aisle, 'What was your aunt's name?'

'Eliza, Eliza Black.'

'I don't think I knew her; did she attend St James'?'

'No, Aunt 'Liza was a devout atheist. She did come and visit a few months ago, whilst doing some research, which I intend to finish for her.' Producing the photograph from his jacket and handing it to the vicar, Morgan added, 'She came to look around, along with a foreign gentleman. Perhaps you can remember.'

'Ah yes, of course. Doctor Black.' The vicar looked around the church cautiously and lowered his voice, 'When I first came to this parish eight years ago, I thought it would be a nice change of pace. I'd been a curate in a busy church in London and my wife is originally from Newton – we thought this would be perfect. Don't get me wrong, it is lovely here and everyone is very nice. I just didn't expect so much of my time to get taken up with resolving disputes around flower rotas.' The vicar winked at Morgan and lowered his voice further still, forcing Morgan to lean closer, 'There were one or two other surprises, which is what Dr Black came to speak to me about. Come with me.'

The vicar stood up and walked towards the front of the church, Morgan followed and once they were outside the vicar continued, in hushed tones, 'I told your aunt and her friend about this because she said it was extremely important and I trusted her to keep it to herself. Her friend, the foreign gentleman, he seemed to already know most of what I'm about to tell you, so filling in the gaps seemed harmless. She promised that she would not include this information in her writings but needed some answers, she believed it was a matter of life and death.'

'Life and death?' Morgan repeated.

'Yes, I don't know how exactly but she was quite insistent.'

'And this is about the meteorites?' Morgan said with a puzzled frown.

'Indeed. As I said, your aunt thought it was very important.'

Adam led Morgan to the thick, wooden door at the back of the church where Eliza and the foreign gentleman had posed for the photograph. 'I wouldn't let your aunt's friend take any pictures inside but I didn't think there was any harm in that photograph,' the vicar explained, looking around carefully, as he produced a large key and unlocked the old door. 'Mind your head as you come in and best close the door behind you.' he instructed, handing Morgan one of two electric torches plucked from an alcove just inside the door.

Morgan followed the cleric down a short flight of steps and into a long passage spanning the width of the church, with simple stone arches interrupting the walls at regular intervals, leading to numerous side rooms. The air was cool and dry and the inky darkness heightened Morgan's other senses.

'I imagine you are aware,' the vicar explained, 'of the witch trials that took place here in the fourteenth century.'

'Yes, I've read about them.' Morgan replied, shining his torch into one of the rooms, which was full of stone sarcophagi and headstones. In other circumstances Morgan would have revelled in the opportunity to explore the crypts thoroughly but Adam's manner made it clear he had something specific to show him.

'The witch trials in the Middle Ages were a highly regrettable period in church history,' Adam continued as he led Morgan through the crypts. 'Fuelled by paranoia, neighbours turned on each other and many innocent people were wrongfully accused of the most ridiculous crimes and tortured and executed in the most horrible ways. It is amongst the greatest crimes in church history. In a few rarer cases, such as Monksford, people were genuinely practicing witchcraft or something that resembled it. These practices included some horrific, blasphemous rituals and rites. Details of exactly what was occurring have been lost because those who witnessed them refused to speak of it - such was the horror.'

'Is this true?' asked Morgan as the vicar turned to face him as they reached another heavy wooden door at the end of the passage.

'I was also dubious when this was all explained to me upon my appointment here but your aunt and her friend confirmed it all to me. The writings and artifacts the locals used in their rituals were brought to the church and locked in the crypts, including a large stone altar.' Adam produced another large key and unlocked the heavy door, pushing it open with no small amount of effort. 'Most of it was seized when Henry VIII's men looted churches for treasure in the fifteen-hundreds but a few pieces remain, including this fragment of the original altar.'

As they entered a small room barely enough to fit the two of them, the vicar shone his torch onto a piece of mottled rock nestled on a stone shelf. Morgan recognised it instantly as being a pallasite, similar in colour and composition to the meteorite sitting in the crater on Dunmoor Hill. 'Is it?' Morgan began, looking at Adam's face, mere inches from his own. The vicar nodded.

'Yes, it's a piece of meteorite.'

Morgan studied it closely, it had the same smooth, cold feel of the larger piece he'd visited the previous night. It was a centimetre thick and roughly triangular; the size of a dinner plate with rough jagged edges as if it had been broken off a larger specimen.

'The altar was smashed apart, somehow,' the cleric explained, 'and the fragments brought here and locked away. This is all that is left.'

'Incredible,' Morgan replied, shining his torch closely and observing how the light reflected and scattered onto the low stone ceiling, 'It is just like the other one.'

Adam drew Morgan's attention to the other objects stored in the room. Several daggers with unusual carvings barely visible beneath layers of rust, a strange metal ball made from twisted strips of iron attached to a short chain and a wooden carving of a catlike animal with long ears and no tail. Adam could offer no explanation as to the origin or purpose of these objects beside his original claim that they were used in some hideous ritual.

After leaving the crypts Adam and Morgan sat on a bench in the church grounds while the vicar filled in the gaps. 'Ever since the trials the priests of this church have been the guardians of these artifacts, protecting them and ensuring they were never used again. The rest of the meteorite pieces were carried away, nobody knows what happened to them. When your aunt found out about the previous meteorite, she asked me if there were any church records about it here. I'm sorry to say that I initially kept the information from her, as the presence of these artifacts here is supposed to be a secret. When she returned with her friend, they explained to me that they believed that since the meteorite fell two years ago, the rituals had begun again. I told them everything I knew and showed them what I have shown you.'

'Do you know anything about these rituals?' Morgan asked.

'Not at all.'

'Did they tell you anything else about the trials that happened here?'

'I'm afraid not. I don't think they knew much themselves, only what I've told you. They said that I should regularly check on the objects and ensure they have not been disturbed. They made me promise to tell no one, a vow I am now breaking but only because I believe it is for the greater good.'

Morgan furrowed his brow.

'Witchcraft is a myth,' the vicar advised, 'It isn't real. If there are a few people chanting and trying to cast spells, what harm is it?'

'You are probably right but if my aunt believed it important enough to come out of retirement and to invite her friend here to help her, then I should carry on investigating.'

'Don't worry yourself. It is most likely nothing to be concerned about.'

'You said that my aunt's friend already knew most of this?'

'Yes, he already knew these things were here and about the history of them – I don't know how, it is supposed to be a closely guarded secret.'

'That is very strange. Did you catch the name of my aunt's friend?'

'Not that I can recall I'm afraid.'

'Was it Dr Zigler?' Morgan asked.

'I don't know. The more I think about it, the stranger it seems. There was something odd about him, if you asked me to describe him, I don't think I could. It's as if, despite remembering our conversations and him being here, the details about himself refused to implant themselves on my brain fully, like a figure from a dream.'

'How strange,' Morgan replied and after a long moment of silence he thanked the vicar for his help, stood up and made his way out of the churchyard.

After lunch Morgan made some notes about his conversation with the vicar, being sure to omit details that could identify the source of his information or the whereabouts of the meteorite fragment and the artifacts. Armed with a cup of tea and his notebook, he sat in the hallway and, using the number his old professor had given him, phoned Miskatonic University in Massachusetts. A woman with a cheery voice and a thick New England accent answered the telephone, 'Miskatonic U. Mandy speaking. How can I help?'

'Good morning,' Morgan said, acknowledging the time difference, 'My name is Doctor Morgan Black. I was hoping to speak to a Dr Zigler, in your history department.'

'Let me put you through to the history faculty office, someone there will be able to help you.'

A short moment later Morgan was connected to the history office, where he introduced himself and repeated his request to speak to Dr Zigler to a woman who sounded identical to the first and claimed to be a professor of history.

'I'm very sorry,' she explained, 'But Dr Zigler passed away a few days ago. Were you a friend of his?'

'Not exactly. My aunt was, she died just over a month ago, and I think he was helping her with some research. Her name was Eliza Black.'

'Dr Eliza Black?' the woman replied enthusiastically, 'I had the privilege of meeting her when she came to speak here about ten years ago, I was a student then. To be honest with you, she is something of a hero of mine, I was very sad to hear about her passing.'

'Oh,' Morgan said, somewhat taken aback, 'That's very kind of you to say so.'

'And yes, if I recall Zigler did make a trip to England a few months ago. I wasn't particularly close to him but I do remember him mentioning it.'

'Is there anything you can tell me about him? I'm trying to continue my aunt's research and his visit seems important.' Morgan asked.

'We were talking about him over lunch yesterday, after we found out what had happened, he'd lived an extraordinary life. Did you know he was nearly ninety? But to look at him you would have guessed he wasn't even fifty.'

'That's incredible and he still worked at the university?'

'Yes, he was a part-time curator of the history archives, came in a couple of times a week to tidy everything up. He used to lecture a long time ago but things changed.'

'What do you mean?' Morgan asked.

'Well, Miskatonic used to have something of a reputation. Some strange things have happened here. The administration decided it was time to move away from certain areas of study, so that the university would be taken more seriously.'

'What did he teach?' Morgan enquired.

'He was an occultist.'

'An occultist? But that's a pseudo-science.'

'That's right, but it used to be taken very seriously. Before the Second World War he'd been an academic in Germany, he travelled around the world and had some important papers published. When Hitler rose to power, he was invited to work on some of the Nazi government's secret projects. Hitler was obsessed with the occult and believed that, with the help of experts, he could summon dark forces to help him win the war.'
'He told you this?'
'Not me personally, he told Marie-Anne, the department head, and she told us about it yesterday. Zelig didn't want to work for the Nazis so he fled and brought as much of his research and artifacts with him as he could. He wound up here and Miskatonic welcomed him with open arms.'
'That is an incredible story. My aunt had known him for a long time but I only met him once when I was a child. I think they met in the sixties in America. What happened to him?'
'He just passed away in his sleep. Was there anything in particular you wanted to talk to him about?' the woman enquired.
'I just thought he might be able to help me fill in a few holes in my aunt's research.'
'Such as?'
'Well, this might seem strange, but I'm looking for a text that my aunt's notes refer to. It seems very

important and each time she references it she just writes the initials AA.'

'AA? Oh. That damned book!' the American professor exclaimed. 'Sorry,' she continued, 'It just causes nothing but problems around here. AA is probably Al-Azif, sometimes called The Necronomicon. Have you heard of it?'

'Just folk stories and horror films,' Morgan replied, 'I always thought it was a myth.'

'No, it's quite real. There's a copy here in the archives. It was moved out of the library when they had the big shake up. Only a few have read it but Dr Zelig was something of an expert, by all accounts. One of the reasons he fled Germany was because he didn't want the Nazis getting their hands on his copy or his notes about it.'

'I see,' Morgan replied, though he still didn't understand fully.

'How much do you know about Al-Azif?' the American professor asked cautiously.

'Not much at all, I'm afraid.'

'Look, I'm no expert but you said that it's important to the research and I'm a big fan of your aunt's work so I'll tell you everything I know, even though we're not really supposed to talk about that book anymore.'

'Thank you. I really appreciate it.'

'It was written in the seven-hundreds in Damascus by an Arab poet named Abdul Alhazred. He was quite well known and travelled all across Arabia, visiting ruins and supposedly magical places. He is alleged to have gone mad and there are all sorts of strange stories about his death. Al Azif became popular with philosophers and alchemists and was translated into Greek and then Latin. Pope Gregory IX banned it and it was suppressed, almost disappearing entirely. Zigler's copy is the only known Arabic copy, which he kept locked in the university archives along with the Latin copy the university already had when he arrived. It makes Miskatonic the only institution in the world with two copies, with the possible exception of the Vatican.

'It's a strange book or so I'm told, I've never read it myself and don't ever intend to. It's full of unusual rituals and magic spells. I have no interest in that sort of thing. The university keeps it under lock and key at all times and no one was allowed access to it, besides Zigler.'

'Well, if that is the source in question, then my aunt must have had a copy somewhere or at least some notes she was working from, though I've not seen it,' Morgan suggested.

'Will you just hold on one moment? I have the box of things from Zigler's desk here. Let me just have a look and see if there's anything helpful.'

The phone clicked as the professor placed it on the desk. Morgan waited patiently and a few minutes later she returned.

'Hi. Are you still there?'

'Yes, I'm here.'

'There's not much to be honest. A few notes, a shopping list and a picture of him as a young man – quite handsome, if I may say. There is a short letter from Dr Black though. It doesn't make much sense but I can read it to you.'

'Yes please.'

'Dearest Fritz, please forgive the briefness of this reply. Thank you kindly for your advice concerning the situation here in Monksford and thank you again for all of your help on your recent visit. It was a pleasure to spend time with you and your guidance has proven extremely useful in this delicate matter. Thank you also for giving me your translation of the book. I have taken your advice and it is now in the safest place with the key hidden in the holiest of holies – as we discussed. I have not heard from Morgan in some time but if the worst should happen and this illness does progress to its inevitable end, I trust that he will be able to continue this work and find a way to stop these people from doing what they are so determined to do. If the worst should happen, I ask that you tell him everything you know when he returns. Yours sincerely Eliza.'

'Thank you, that is incredibly helpful.'
'You are most welcome and if there's anything else I can do please feel free to call.'
'Thank you.'
The phone clicked and Morgan sat in the hallway listening to the dialling tone for several long minutes as he collected his thoughts and attempted to decide on his next steps in solving the strange mystery that had consumed him.

Seven:

Morgan spent the remainder of Wednesday and most of Thursday searching his aunt's house for her copy of the fabled grimoire. If Al-Azif was the missing source document, he had surmised, then by reading it he would finally understand the significance of the meteorites to Monksford's history and the reason his aunt had been researching the matter with such urgency.

He spent Wednesday evening searching with frenetic energy, like a man possessed and only stopped upon discovering a shoebox of letters underneath Liza's bed. At first, he thought he had found the object he was looking for, but instead found something of a different type of value entirely. The letters were all from him to his Aunt and dated as far back as his first few weeks as an undergraduate, all the way through to his recent trip to Central Africa.

He thumbed through them, stopping to read one that looked more interesting. It was a real insight into his own past anxieties and he could remember her wise replies to his concerns about fitting in with his privately educated peers, struggling to find research materials or feeling the pressure ahead of exams. His eyes filled with tears as he read some of his letters from Africa, which were few and far between. He knew that his aunt was always excited to hear from him but had no idea she had treasured the letters so much, even if she was unable to reply due to his lack of return address during his expedition.

Morgan sat quietly for a long time on the bedroom floor as the weight of his grief and the realisation that he would never see his aunt again finally hit him.

Thursday was hot and humid and filled with the sound of Tom mowing the grass in the garden. He toyed with asking him if his aunt had mentioned anything about the book but it seemed unlikely, so he simply waved from the window as he searched. He decided to take a more systematic approach to searching that on the previous day and moved from room to room, carefully moving furniture in order to check every nook and cranny. His efforts were fruitless and as the weather outside became more oppressive his searching became increasingly frantic.

Morgan was searching the garden shed, the most unlikely place he could think of, when the heavens finally broke. He had barely noticed the rumbles of thunder but now that rain was falling in sheets, he regretted walking to the shed without shoes. He sheltered in the shed for a while, watching the rain and waiting for it to ease, as he thought about the letter Aunt 'Liza had written to

Dr Zigler. Who was Eliza referring to when she said "these people" and what was it they were so determined to do? 'She hid the book in the "safest place",' he said to himself, 'with the key in the "holiest of holies". What does that mean?'.

When it became clear that the rain would not ease and, if anything, was growing heavier, Morgan decided to brave the storm for the few seconds it would take him to cross the garden and return to the house. He ran as swiftly as his bare feet would allow, while attempting to dodge the worst puddles, but still managed to find himself thoroughly soaked when he reached the kitchen. He took himself upstairs, peeled his clothes off and dried himself with a towel before getting changed. As he was pulling on a fresh shirt, he heard a loud knock on the front door. Puzzled by who would be calling round during a storm he quickly descended the stairs and answered.

A young police woman stood in the doorway. She looked thoroughly soaked, her short blonde hair so wet that it stuck to the side of her face. Without hesitation, Morgan invited her into the hallway where water from her uniform dripped onto the wooden floor. 'I'm sorry,' she said, looking down at the puddle now forming at her feet.
'Don't worry,' Morgan replied, 'I've just come in from outside so I need to mop up anyway. What can I do for you?'

The officer took off her peaked hat, her hair a mess beneath it. Morgan offered her the towel that was still in his hands, which she gratefully took and patted her hair and face dry with before handing it back.

'It's rather unpleasant I'm afraid, but a schoolgirl has gone missing in the village and I'm going door to door asking if anyone has seen her.' She produced a school photo in a cardboard frame, carefully wrapped in a plastic wallet, from her jacket and handed it to Morgan.

Morgan looked at it carefully, 'I haven't seen her, I'm afraid. When did she go missing?'

'No one has seen her since this morning. She left for school but never arrived. None of her friends know where she is. Her parents only noticed when she didn't return from school.'

'I'm sorry, I've been in the house all day. How old is she?'

'Sixteen.'

'Oh dear. I hope she's okay. I'm sorry I can't help you.' Morgan said sincerely.

'Thank you for your time,' the police officer replied, 'If you hear or see anything do not hesitate in calling the police.' She returned the photo to her jacket, 'Sorry about the mess,' she said, gesturing at the wet floor.

'It's okay,' Morgan said, 'You must be freezing. I was just about to make a hot drink. Do you want one?'

The police woman hesitated, 'I wouldn't mind a coffee, if that's okay? This is my last house before I'm due back at the station. My name is Julie.'

Morgan smiled, 'I'm Morgan.' He took her coat and hat and hung them up before leading her into the kitchen. 'Sorry about the mess, it's my late aunt's house and I've been sorting through things.'

'I'm sorry about your aunt, were you close?'

'Yes,' Morgan replied, 'She raised me from the age of ten.'

Julie offered her sympathies again as Morgan handed her a cup of hot, black coffee.

'It's a nice house. Did you grow up here?' She enquired.

'I did, yeah. Are you local?'

'I grew up just down the road in Dunton.'

Morgan sat down in the seat opposite her and smiled. 'How long have you been in the police?'

'I'm new, just a few months. I probably shouldn't be doing this.'

'I'm sure it's fine. What happened with this missing girl?'

'Catherine Brown. She's just turned sixteen. She didn't come home from school today so her parents called around her friends. That's when they found out that she hadn't even gone to school

today. The school didn't think anything of it because she quite regularly truants but none of the friend she normally goes with haven't seen her today either. That's when they called the police.'
'I hope she's okay, especially out in the storm.'

The evening light began to fade as the storm wore on, while Morgan and Julie chatted and drank their hot beverages. As she explained how she came to join the police, Morgan's eyes wandered past the pretty young police officer and into the hallway behind her. From his vantage point he could see a small section of the open doorway to the living room and the far corner of the mantlepiece beyond. On top of the mantlepiece, just about the only object visible in the other room, was the framed picture of him and his aunt in Jerusalem. The words "Temple Mount" rattled around his head for a long moment while Julie told him about the officers conducting the door-to-door enquiries in several nearby villages.

Jerusalem. Temple Mount. He couldn't make out the photo from where he sat but he knew it well. The Dome of the Rock, the great mosque built on the site of the Temple in Jerusalem was directly behind them. They were both smiling, despite the sweat dripping from their brows. It had been a very hot day and they had been walking around the streets of Jerusalem for several hours.

'What do you do?' Julie asked Morgan.

'I'm a historian and archaeologist. I've recently got back from an expedition in Africa.' As he roughly explained his part in the search for the lost Bantu city, his thoughts drifted to the letter his aunt had sent Dr Zigler. "The safest place". Where was the safest place to hide an important book? "The Holiest of Holies".

'I'd better go,' Julie interrupted, 'But it's been nice chatting. Shall we do it again sometime?'

Morgan smiled, 'Sure, are you free for lunch sometime?'

'I'm not working tomorrow.'

'Do you know Giovani's? Italian place in Newton?'

'Yes.'

'Shall we meet there are 1?'

'That sounds good.'

Before she left, Julie gave Morgan her phone number, which he left on the table in the hallway. He handed her coat and hat to her and she put them on before stepping out into the rain and walking back down the lane. Morgan watched her disappear from sight before closing the door firmly and all but running into the living room and to the mantlepiece, where he picked up the picture.

'The Holiest of Holies,' he said to himself, turning it around and carefully removing the back of the frame. Sure enough, folded neatly behind the picture was a piece of paper and a key. The piece of paper contained a string of numbers and the address of a bank in Newton. Morgan chuckled, the Holiest of Holies was a room in the temple in Jerusalem, she must have included it in the later so that Dr Zigler or Morgan could find the key to a safety deposit box – the safest place – should anything happen to her. He scolded himself for taking the whole day to solve such a simple riddle and decided he would go to the bank first thing in the morning to retrieve the missing book before the weekend.

The storm that harassed Monksford lasted well into the night but by the morning, when Morgan took a bus into Newton, it had long cleared. The summer morning sun reflected brightly on the wet roads all the way into town. Morgan squinted out of the window in thought, wondering just what details could be hidden in a legendary text written twelve-hundred years ago in Arabia that had so illuminated his aunt's research into the history of a small village in England.

Morgan was disappointed to find that, despite his early arrival, there were other customers also waiting for the bank to open. Morgan took his place in the queue and waited patiently. When it was finally his turn he stepped forward, armed with the safety-deposit-box number and key from the picture, his passport, a letter from his Aunt's solicitor and a copy of his

Aunt's death certificate – all he believed necessary to prove himself the new legal owner of the safe's contents. The bank clerk was polite and efficient and soon Morgan was in a small room with the box, which he tentatively opened.

Morgan wasn't sure exactly what he had expected to find. He knew that it was Zigler's handwritten translation, rather than an old Arabic text, inside the box. However, with all the hushed legends around Al Azif, the so-called Necronomicon, as well as the importance his aunt seemed to place in it, he found the grimoire itself somewhat disappointing. An old leather-bound notepad, pages slightly yellowed but otherwise in good condition, small but thick – like a pocket Bible. On the front, scratched into the leather was a twisted five-pointed star – which Morgan instantly recognised as matching the one he'd seen on the meteorite itself. He opened a random page and read Zigler's small but neat handwriting:

"That is dead which can eternal lie. And with strange aeons, even death may die."

Morgan shuddered involuntarily and closed the book, placing it carefully inside his shoulder bag, along with the other notes he had brought with him.

Morgan spoke to the clerk to ensure that the safe, now empty, would still be available to him when he wished to return the book and took himself to the canal, sat on a bench and began to read the cursed text.

Eight:

Giovani's was something of an institution in Newton. A light and breezy Italian café that had passed from father to son and served traditional Italian food at a good price. Chequered plastic table cloths, faded photographs of the Sicilian countryside and a pleasing aroma emanating from the kitchen all contributed to the friendly atmosphere that was enhanced further by Giovani Junior's effervescent smile and infectious laughter. Rumour had it that his father had come to Britain in order to escape the mafia, Morgan imagined the same rumour existed about every Sicilian family in the country. Giovani recognised him instantly and greeted him warmly, sharing his condolences and asking him about his time in Africa. Morgan responded by enquiring after Giovani's father, who had become increasingly infirm in his old age. Giovani sat Morgan at the window, brought him a coffee. 'I won't eat just yet,' Morgan explained, 'I'm waiting for someone.'

Morgan was consumed by reading the Necronomicon and scratching notes into his pad when Julie walked in. He was struggling to make any connection between the text and his Aunt's research into the history of Monksford. The descriptions of ancient deities and horrific rituals made him feel uncomfortable and seemed to have little bearing on his research so far. He was in the middle of reading a prophecy concerning the return of chaos to the world when Julie came and sat opposite him.

'Sorry,' Morgan said, closing the book and putting it in his bag, 'I didn't see you come in.'

'That's alright,' Julie smiled, 'What are you reading?'

'It's a translation of an old text given to my Aunt. She was writing a book about the history of Monksford, but this doesn't seem to have anything to do with it.'

'Your Aunt was a historian too?' Julie enquired.

'Yeah, she's the reason I got into it, archaeology, anthropology and everything. She was an expert in medieval Britain though, whereas I studied ancient fertility cults.'

A young woman approached the table and took Morgan and Julie's food orders. Morgan ordered a carbonara and Julie ordered gnocchi.

'How did you end up living with her?' Julie asked.

'My mum was a hippie, I lived on a commune until I was about 8 when I was taken into care. A couple of years later I ended up with my Aunt.'

'What happened to your Mum? If you don't mind me asking.'

Morgan looked down at the table for a moment before responding. 'She was taking lots of drugs, hallucinogens I guess, and they did something to her brain and she lost herself. She's in psychiatric care, she doesn't know who anyone is anymore and mostly just talks nonsense.'

'I'm sorry, I didn't mean to bring up something so painful.'

'It's okay,' Morgan replied, 'I'm just not used to talking about it. I haven't seen her in years. I went in before my expedition but she didn't know who I was, she doesn't understand what is happening around her. I try not to think about it.'

Julie reached over and put her hand on Morgan's, 'It's okay, let's talk about something else.'

Morgan nodded and slowly drew back his hand, 'So,' he pondered, 'Why did you become a police officer?'

'My father and brother are both in the police. I wanted to help people and it seemed the best way.'

The two chatted and ate together quite comfortably, exchanging stories from their very different careers and enjoying each other's company. They managed to forget about meteorites, ancient rituals and missing girls for a couple of hours, following up lunch with a walk through the market and along the canal. Julie gave Morgan a lift back to Monksford and they shared an awkward goodbye outside the cottage and arranged to see each other again soon.

As he was walking down the garden path, Morgan heard Tom whistling in the neighbouring garden.

'Afternoon, Mr Cartwright.'

'Afternoon, my boy,' the old gentleman replied, 'And I've told you before, call me Tom. Mr Cartwright was my father.'

'Sorry Tom. You not down the pub today?'

' 'fraid not. She's banned me from going until I've done the weeding. Hid my wallet, would you believe?'

Morgan chuckled.

'How's your research going?' Tom asked.

'Not bad, I've found a source my Aunt was using but I can't make much sense of it.'

'I see,' Tom replied, though he gave the impression he did not fully comprehend.

'Mr Cart -, sorry, Tom, do you ever get the impression something weird is going on in Monksford?'

The old man paused for a long moment, 'You talking about that missing girl?'

'Not specifically. It's just, since I've got here, I don't know, something doesn't seem right.'

'I know what you mean. There's a lot of strange folk about. I've never lived anywhere where so few people go to church on a Sunday.'

Morgan suppressed another chuckle, 'I think that's just the times. People aren't as interested in God anymore.'

Tom shook his head, 'People are always interested in gods – just not necessarily the Christian one.'

At that moment, a shrill yell rang out from the open door of the Cartwright's cottage, followed seconds later my Mrs Cartwright.

'Tom, Tom. Will you come in here please? There's a spider in the kitchen again,' she shrieked, before seeing Morgan and attempting to appear more composed, 'Oh, sorry Morgan, I didn't see you there. How are you?'

'Very well, thank you,' Morgan replied.

'I'd best go, see you soon,' Tom said, rising from his weeds and heading indoors followed by Mrs Cartwright, whose instructions on the removal of the spider could still be heard in the garden.

Morgan smiled to himself as he headed up the path, towards his Aunt's cottage. He made himself a cup of tea and sat in the garden with the handwritten copy of *Al-Azif*, flicking through the cursed text in the late afternoon sunshine. As he perused the small volume, he found a small piece of card between two pages, presumably used by his Aunt to mark out a particular page, where a short paragraph had been carefully underlined in pencil.

"His followers claim that the blood of the innocent must pour forth, theirs is the only sacrifice that can appease the Great One, the cursed creature from the stars, the Bringer of Chaos. On the night of the high day, the last day before the sun's retreat, by the light of the full moon on the altar that came to us from the Great One, the Harbinger of Doom, the creature who sleeps in the stars, the sacrifice must be made. Only thus can the Age of Chaos, when the Great One returns and takes dominion over the Empires of the Earth, be achieved."

Morgan furrowed his brow, wondering if it was his Aunt or Dr Zelig who was responsible for marking out this segment of text and what relevance, if any, it had to the history of Monksford.

    He continued to read for some time, finding himself drawn to the scratchy handwriting. Before long he began to feel the books diabolical effect on his mind as the edges of his perception started to fray. He jumped at shadows moving softly in the breeze, haunted by the stirrings of a neighbour's cat on the lawn. The tendrils of chaos began to permeate his consciousness with images of forgotten rituals and a maniacal mythos of unspeakable horror.

    His musings were interrupted by the rattling of the side gate. He turned around to see Shirley appear out of the shadows and into the back garden. She looked radiant in a bright yellow summer dress, that contrasted well with her dark hair and tanned complexion.

'Sorry I'm so early, I thought we could have a drink here before we go,' she said as she walked towards Morgan.

'Go where?' he enquired.

'To the pub, you said you'd come tonight.'

'Oh yes, of course,' Morgan fumbled, 'I forgot about that.'

Shirley sat down and produced a bottle of wine from her bag with an almost magical flourish.

'I'll get some glasses.'

When Morgan returned to the garden with a plate of cheese, pate and crackers, a corkscrew and two mugs, Shirley was flicking through Dr Zelig's book.

'I couldn't find any wine glasses, will these do?'

Shirley chuckled, 'Of course,' as he opened the wine and poured into each of their mugs. Morgan handed her a mug and offered her something to eat.

'This is a strange little book,' Shirley commented, 'Where did you get it?'

'Someone gave it to Aunt 'Liza, I'm not really sure why.'

'They will arrive from above in rock and fire,' Shirley read aloud. *'We will pay them worship and they will*

cleanse the Earth – those creatures of chaos. They will give us our world back.'

Shirley looked at Morgan, a puzzled look on her face. 'This is morbid,' she added, closing the book and placing in back on the table and picking up a piece of cheese instead, 'Have you seen your mum since you got back?'

'No,' Morgan replied, a sad look on his face. 'Apparently, she doesn't really talk to anyone anymore and when she does it is just gibberish.'

Shirley placed a hand on his arm as he paused.

'I visited her before I went away and she didn't even know who I was.'

'That must have been horrible.'

Morgan nodded. 'Can we change the subject?' he asked.

'How's everything else going?' Shirley responded, looking around the garden.

Morgan sighed, 'My research has hit a brick wall, to be honest. I can't understand what my Aunt was trying to find out and this place,' he gestured towards the cottage, 'I don't know what to do with it.'

'No?'

'I'm not sure I want to stay in Monksford but if I sell up then it won't be Aunt 'Liza's cottage anymore, it will be someone else's and I don't like the thought of that.'

'I know what you mean. Where do you think you'll go?'

'I don't know. The researcher in charge of our expedition in Africa wants to go back but it could be years before the civil war is over. In the meantime, I could try and find a lecture job somewhere.'

'Try not to disappear for so long this time,' Shirley replied.

'I won't and I'll definitely go somewhere where it's easier to write.'

'And somewhere with a return address.'

'Definitely,' Morgan said with a smile, as he refilled their mugs.

Nine:

The sun was just hanging above the trees of Prince's Wood when Shirley and Morgan arrived at the Devil's Due in her Volkswagen van. The sounds of music and merriment filled the air as they crossed the carpark in search of Shirley's friends. Sunset was still a couple of hours away and the warm evening sunshine meant that many of the pub's patrons gathered outside. A small stage was set up against the wall of the barn, where a four-piece band were warming up.

Shirley and Morgan stepped aside at the gate to the garden to allow a troupe of Morris Dancers to trot past in a cacophony of bells. Two men in white robes nudged each other and leered over Shirley as she walked past in her yellow dress.
'What on Earth?' Morgan muttered.
'It's solstice,' Shirley replied with a grin, 'Don't you remember?'
'Of course,' Morgan nodded, 'I'm glad we missed the Morris-men.'

Shirley's friends were gathered on a couple of benches, close to the pub's entrance. Morgan grimaced inwardly at the sight of Shelly and her boyfriend Pat. The only other man in the large group was Geoff, who he had known at school and, although a little dull, was not unpleasant company.

Morgan offered to buy a round but everyone had full glasses, so he headed inside to buy drinks for him and Shirley.

When Morgan returned, the animated group conversation fell silent. He took a seat in the empty space next to Shirley and surveyed the eight faces around him, the awkward reticence in sharp contrast to the revelry around them.

'How was Africa?' Geoff enquired, finally breaking through the invisible curtain that had descended on the group.

'It was interesting,' Morgan replied, 'very hot and lots of insects.'

Geoff's reply was drowned out by the band striking up to play their first number.

Morgan nursed his shandy and remained on the fringes of the evening's discussions, occasionally conversing briefly with Shirley and Geoff, who had a lot of questions about Morgan's time in Africa. The group laughed as they discussed the latest gossip – mostly about people Morgan barely knew and he was content to remain out of the limelight.

Eventually, after some extended whispering and inspired by the alcohol coursing through their veins, some members of the group broke off and began to
dance together or with members of other groups. The awkwardness that surrounded Morgan's

arrival had all but dissipated when the intoxicated Shelly, an old friend of Shirley's, returned to the table with two others and attempted to initiate a drinking game.

'What you have to do,' she explained, 'is say something that you have never done. Then everyone around the table who has done it, has to drink.'

Shirley glanced at Morgan and surreptitiously rolled her eyes.

'Here we go,' Shelly continued, 'I have never kissed a member of the same sex.'

The other people around the table glanced at each other but nobody took a drink.

Shelly's friend took over, 'I have never been so drunk I can't remember anything.'

One or two members of the group glanced at each other with a chuckle and took a drink. Morgan sighed and began to rise from his seat.

'Where are you going Morgan?' Shelly asked, 'Don't you want to play?'

Morgan stole a look at Shirley, who screwed her face in confusion.

'I've got one just for you,' Shelly said, with a cruel grin, 'I have never told someone I love them six months before their wedding and then disappeared half way across the world.'

The group fell silent.

'Come on Morgan, aren't you going to drink?' Shelly laughed.

Morgan looked down into the dregs of his second shandy and turned towards Shirley, 'I,' he hesitated, 'I think I should go.' Without waiting for a response, he rose from his seat and strode across the pub garden towards the carpark.

Just as he passed through the gate, he felt a hand on his elbow and looked over his shoulder to see Shirley behind him.

'Don't go,' she said.

'I think it's probably best.'

'Shelly's just drunk and being needlessly cruel. Please stay a little longer.'

Morgan sighed and let Shelly lead him across the car park to a large log by the entrance to the woods, which they sat on together.

'I'm really sorry about her,' Shirley said after a long moment of quiet.

'You don't have to apologise for your friend,' Morgan replied.

'Well, somebody has to. I don't know why I spend time with her, she's never been a particularly nice person.'

'She's just looking out for you. She obviously blames me for you and Ken breaking up. Maybe she's right. I shouldn't have disappeared the way I did.'

'Morgan,' Shirley sighed, 'You hardly disappeared. That was a trip that had been months in the planning. It wasn't your fault that it went on so much longer than expected or that a civil war cut you off from the outside world for so long.'
Morgan attempted to respond but was cut off.
'And, as for me and Ken, Shelly has no idea why we broke up. They might be cousins but she doesn't have a clue.'
'Still,' Morgan insisted, 'I am sorry.'
'Morgan,' Shirley sighed deeply, 'You are my best friend and I've missed you terribly. When the letters stopped, I was worried about you. I used to go round your Aunt's and speak to her, to find out if she'd heard anything. When the odd message came through, I was delighted. It was horrible not being able to write back, there were so many things I wanted to be able to talk to you about.' Tears began to roll down Shirley's soft cheeks, 'You were the only person I could talk to and you were gone.' Morgan put his arms around Shirley and held her close, 'I'm so sorry,' he repeated.

He held her for a long moment and listened to the dissonant mix of evening birdsong and the music from the pub garden. After a few moments, Shirley gently wriggled free and Morgan released her. She looked up at him and smiled sadly, 'I'm sorry, Morgan,' she said, 'It's my fault.'
Morgan furrowed his brow.

'I told Shelly and the others that Ken and I broke up because of you. Well, they assumed it was because of you and I let them believe it.'

'I don't understand,' Morgan replied.

'But that isn't why I left him. I found out something, something people around here would never understand. You know how backwards this place is.'

Morgan, brow still furrowed, was beginning to understand.

'I've never told anyone this before,' Shirley continued, looking up at Morgan's kind eyes, 'I'm a lesbian.'

Morgan smiled, 'Come here,' he said as he hugged her close to him again. 'That's amazing.' He laughed, 'I'm really happy for you.'

'But, don't you think it's weird or wrong or something?'

'Not really,' Morgan smiled, 'Besides, I always suspected Aunt 'Liza might have been one too.'

'Yeah?'

'Maybe.'

Shirley reflected Morgan's grin, 'I'm sorry I used you as a shield.'

'It's okay. I know what people around here are like. You've always been my best friend – I don't mind being a shield for you.'

Ten:

Shirley and Morgan sat on the log together for a while. Shirley drank wine from a bottle given to them by an inebriated Morris dancer, whilst Morgan contented himself with another shandy. The tears of earlier had given away to laughter.
'How long have you known?' Morgan enquired.
'I don't know. There's been something there for a long time but I didn't know what it was. Do you remember that girl you were at university with? Kim?'
'Yeah, I remember her.'
'Well, I was infatuated with her for a long time, I only met her three or four times but couldn't stop thinking about her. I think that was the start of it.'
'Have you had any girlfriends?'
'Not really,' Shirley replied, 'I went on a few dates a couple of years back, when I was in London a lot for work, but not since I've been stuck here all the time.'
Morgan nodded sympathetically.
'It's like you said the other day,' Shirley continued, 'I need to get away from this place. It's old fashioned, full of people like Shelly and girls disappearing every Summer.'
'Girls?' Morgan asked, puzzled.

'Yeah, didn't you see in the papers? A teenage girl has gone missing?'
'I know that, but you said girls. Plural.'
'Yes,' Shirley replied, finishing the last of the wine, 'One went missing last year too.'
Morgan furrowed his brow in thought for a moment, 'How strange.'
'Sorry, I didn't mean to bring the mood down. It's such a beautiful evening.'
'It really is,' Morgan replied.
'And where else has its own meteorite?' Shirley chuckled, her head swimming pleasantly between the wine and the fading heat of the sun.
'Well, that's definitely something.' Morgan sighed.
'Two years today.'
'What is?'
'The meteor landing. Two years today.' Shirley repeated. *'That cursed rock.'*
Morgan furrowed his brow, 'What did you say?'
'That cursed rock. From the strange book you were reading. It was about the meteorite, wasn't it?'
Shirley let the bottle fall gently to the dirt floor, as the lights suddenly came on in Morgan's head. 'I need to make a phone call.'

The Volkswagen van hurtled down country lanes, with Morgan at the wheel and Shirley drunkenly giving directions from the passenger seat. He had long since given up trying to explain the situation to her, instead simply insisting that they needed to get up to Dunmoor Hill as quickly as possible.

Julie's car was already in the layby opposite the telephone box when Morgan and Shirley arrived. When the Volkswagen's engine stopped, Julie stepped out of her car and walked over. She looked at Shirley, who was all but asleep in the passenger seat, and threw Morgan a puzzled look.

'This is Shirley, my oldest friend, we were in the pub when-'

'Are you insured to drive this van?' Julie interrupted.

'I don't know,' Morgan stammered, 'You can arrest me later. It's about the missing girl.'

'Yes, you said on the phone you know where she is.'

'They've taken her up to the crater. They're going to sacrifice her on the meteorite.'

'Who is?'

'I don't know,' Morgan replied, 'It's a cult. They worship chaos and think the meteorite is an altar. It's what my aunt had been studying, it's what happened to the girl who went missing last summer. We have to stop them before they kill her.'

Without further question Julie handed Morgan a powerful police issue torch. 'Start heading up,' she told him, 'I'll grab my police gear from the car and call for backup from the phone box and catch you up.'

Morgan nodded and, leaving Shirley asleep in the van, began walking up the footpath towards the scorched woodland and the crater that would house the obscene ceremony.

He kept the heavy torch switched off, preferring to navigate by the light of the full moon and concerned that the bright electric light would reduce his peripheral vision and draw unwanted attention to his approach. He did not know if any cult members were aware of either his or his aunt's investigations into the Monksford underworld. He had not been discrete in discussing his research with Tom in the pub and the priest had warned him of the strange characters in the village. It was entirely possible that his arrival was expected or that there were people hiding in the woods with the intention of preventing anyone from interrupting the ritual.

The woods were silent, except for the occasional cry of an owl or the distant churring of a nightjar, sounds that would normally delight Morgan, but tonight the ventriloquial melodies gave him no comfort. Instead, he fiddled with the hardbound notebook in his jacket pocket. His aunt had kept it secreted away in a bank vault and now he foolishly carried the dangerous tome into the lair of those with whom it would do the most harm.

He scolded himself for being so slow to realise the true meaning of all that had happened since he had returned to Monksford. He had been spent too much time caught up in the nostalgia of being home and in his desire to redeem himself for being away when his aunt had needed him the most, that he now feared his failure would cost a young woman her life.

The crack of a stick snapping echoed in the stillness and Morgan froze, glancing furtively in every direction for the source of the interruption. For a long moment there was only silence, before the soft thud of boots and the emerging luminance of electric torchlight made its way up the path behind him. Morgan turned and heard Julie's distant voice shouting his name. Morgan flicked on the torch and responded to the call and within moments the pair were reunited.

'Three units are on the way,' the police officer told him, 'This had better not be a hoax or I am in for it.'

'The more I think about it, the more convinced I am that I'm right.'

'Well, you'd better explain it to me then,' Julie reiterated as they continued up the path.

'Hundreds of years ago, in the Middle Ages,' Morgan began, 'another meteorite landed close to Monksford – maybe even in the same place. I don't know how or why, but the locals began to revere it, believing it to be the sign of a pact with some ancient deity, one of the creatures of chaos described in a book called Al Azif, sometimes called the Necronomicon.'

'This sounds crazy,' Julie commented.

'I know but hear me out. They began to make sacrifices and whilst the rest of the country suffered great misfortune, Monksford prospered. They believed this was the work of the ancient deity who sent the meteorite.

'Eventually, the practices here caught the attention of the Catholic church. They suppressed it, removing the meteorite and taking it far away – with the exception of a small piece hidden in the vaults of the local church. Those involved in the rituals were put to death in the so-called witch trials.

'The centuries go by and this has mostly been forgotten, except by a few locals who kept the legends alive, though the details have changed over time. Two years ago, another meteorite fell and the rituals have been revived somehow. Last year they sacrificed that poor girl and this year they intend to sacrifice another, unless we stop them.'

After a brief moment of silence, Julie stopped walking and sighed heavily, 'Are you sure about this?'

Morgan turned to face her, 'Yes. Absolutely. Come on, we need to get up there in case the police don't arrive in time.'

He turned back around and continued walking only for his legs to suddenly freeze beneath him after only a couple of steps. Morgan's whole body convulsed in pain as he slumped to the ground, looking up to see Julie stood over him holding a strange device in her hand as he unsuccessfully tried to fight off the blackness closing in around him.

Eleven:

The darkness around him, combined with the ringing inside his head, meant it took Morgan a long time to realise that he was fully conscious again. His wrists and ankles were bound with something thin and strong and he was propped against a metal wall. He coughed hard and the sound reverberated through the stale air around him. He pulled against his restraints but they were unrelenting and he swore to himself.

'Is there someone there?' a voice enquired in the darkness.

'Yes,' Morgan replied, his mouth dry but for the faint metallic taste of blood.

'Can you help me?' the woman replied, her voice strained and desperate.

'I would if I could but my hands and feet are bound.'

'Mine too.'

'Who are you?' Morgan asked, despite already knowing the answer.

'My name's Mary. They took me a few days ago. I don't know what they want.'

'It's okay Mary,' Morgan said, hoping his voice did not betray his lack of confidence, 'Help is on the way.'

Shirley tried to fight off the alcohol induced slumber and focus on the voices around her.

'We have to stop them before they kill her.'

She recognised Morgan's voice and forced herself to listen. He brought her up here for a reason, she remembered, he said it was important.

'I'll grab my police gear from the car and call for backup from the phone box.'

She didn't recognise the woman's voice and wondered who it could be before she found herself drifting into sleep again, her body slumping forward against the seatbelt

A slamming door brought her to and she watched Morgan disappear into the woods. The woman was walking away from the van, towards the car parked in front of them. She opened the boot and rummaged around for a while before closing it and proceeding over the style and up the path. Shirley shook her head and glanced across the road at the phone box. Its little light shone pathetically against the darkness.

'Something is wrong,' she told herself as she unclipped her seatbelt.

Her foot struck an object in the passenger footwell, she looked down at the squat metal cylinder rolling on the floor between her feet and sighed. She lent down, picked up the object, unscrewed it, took a deep breath and poured the cold coffee down her throat.

'Do you know where we are?' Morgan asked Mary.
'In a van, apart from that I don't know.'
Morgan paused for a moment to ensure that his head, still ringing from the attack, had not been deceived. The silence and stillness gave away that the van was stationary. 'Have we moved since they put me in here?'
'No.'
'Good, that means we're close by. Keep talking, I'm going to try to find you. Maybe we can help each other get free.'

Morgan shuffled awkwardly through the blackness, towards the girl's voice, until he bumped into her feet. Eventually, they managed to move around each other and sit back-to-back. He attempted to pull at her restraints but could not break the cable tie holding her wrists together, neither was she able to help him. Morgan could hear her crying softly as they tried and failed to break free.
'Don't worry,' he reassured her, 'We'll get out of here.'
'They're going to kill me,' she told him, 'I know it.'
'No, they're not. The police know where we are and are on their way.' He hoped he was telling the truth; he was still confused by the attack and unsure of Julie's role in everything. She's a police

officer, he reminded himself, she can't be involved in this.

Suddenly, the van filled with light as the door swung open. Two silhouettes holding torches stood outside whilst two other men stepped into the van. Mary screamed as one of them pulled out a knife and cut the plastic around her ankles and pulled her to her feet. She tried to wriggle free but they hauled her out of the van as Morgan shouted at them to let her go. The door slammed shut, plunging Morgan back into darkness. 'At least I know where the door is now,' he said to himself as he shuffled across the van.

He turned around, pushed his shoulders against the cold metal and managed to slowly lift himself until he was propped up against the door. He felt around for a locking mechanism and, finding a small handle, twisted it. Nothing. Unsurprisingly, the door had been modified to prevent it being unlocked from the inside.

Morgan slumped to the floor and considered his next move carefully. Turning around and laying on his back, he attempted to kick the van door with no success. He persisted for several long minutes until he was out of breath, with the door remaining firmly closed. Despair was rapidly creeping into the corners of his mind. In the darkness and solitude his sense of time was already beginning to ebb away. He couldn't tell how long it had been since

Mary had been taken. Five minutes? Twenty? An hour? He knew the ritual would take some time but had no idea at what point Mary would be sacrificed. The chances of anyone stopping it were rapidly diminishing and he began to wonder what would become of him when the cultists had finished their revelries. He closed his eyes against the darkness and tried desperately to think of a way out of the van, to no avail. He almost laughed as he resigned himself to the situation. He'd survived a civil war in central Africa, only to come back home and find himself kidnapped by chaos worshipping lunatics in the village of his youth. Worse still, he told himself, he had failed to comprehend the gravity of the situation in time to save the life of a young woman. If, somehow, he managed to survive the night, that knowledge would surely haunt him for the rest of his life.

A strange creaking interrupted Morgan's increasingly morbid thoughts. What started as a low scratching rose in volume and pitch to become the unmistakable sound of straining metal. With a sudden pop the door burst open and the dim light of the moon flooded the van. A silhouette with a crowbar in hand cast a long shadow as Morgan's eyes adjusted to the sudden illumination of the world around him. Shirley's voice cut through the silence, 'Morgan. Thank God.'

'Shirley?'

'Morgan. I've had some coffee but I'm still quite drunk.'

Shirley produced a penknife from her pocket and cut the cable ties from Morgan's wrists and ankles as she explained all that had happened. 'I heard Julie say she was going to phone someone but when I saw she hadn't, I called the police and followed her up. I saw her shock you and some people came down and carried you up here. I followed and waited until no one was around, found this,' she gestured towards the crowbar, 'and got you out.'

'Did you see where they took the girl?' Morgan asked.

'Some men came and took her down towards the crater.'

'We need to help her,' Morgan said, finally free of the ties, 'Let's go.'

Shirley and Morgan peered over the precipice of the crater at the scene unfolding below them. A cluster of hooded figures were gathered around the meteorite, which was adorned with candles, chanting in some forgotten language. Morgan counted sixteen figures; a task made difficult by their identical clothing. The two largest held Mary firmly in place before the altar, whilst the other fourteen began a slow procession around the altar as the chant became louder and more complex.

One cultist broke formation in front of the young woman and lifted a long sword horizontally above his head, its hilt glinting fiercely in the candlelight. He knelt down and placing the weapon on the ground, began pouring jars of various liquids over it whilst repeatedly intoning a strange, deep note.

'We've got to do something,' Morgan said, turning to Shirley, 'We need to distract them.'

'I think,' Shirley paused, her face taking on a hint of green, 'I think I'm going to be sick.'

Shirley's loud retching silenced the chanters, who looked up towards them. 'That's good,' he whispered, 'keep going.'

'I can't help it,' she replied, vomiting on the floor beside them.

Morgan ducked low and moved cautiously around the crater, away from the approaching hoods, clutching the cold metal of the crowbar. Manoeuvring himself carefully, he silently descended towards the makeshift altar, keeping out of the eyeline of the men guarding Mary. The guards were shouting instructions up to the hooded figures who were climbing the crater in search of Shirley.

Suddenly, just as she was about the be discovered, Shirley ran out of her hiding place and knocked over the nearest figure with a shove. The three nearest gave pursuit, chasing her up out of the crater just as Morgan was closing in on the meteorite.

Sneaking up behind the nearest guard, grateful that the hoods limited their field of vision, Morgan raised the crowbar above his head and readied himself. He swung the piece of metal down with a thud. The guard fell to his knees, swore loudly and clutched his head. The other guard released Mary in shock as he spun around to face Morgan. 'Run!' Morgan shouted at Mary, who gave flight instantly.

The guard lunged at Morgan but he jumped back, swung the crowbar in a low arc that took him off balance and caused him to stumble slightly. The large figure seized the advantage and charged into Morgan, bundling him off his feet. The crowbar struck the ground with a clang as Morgan attempted to wriggle out of the grasp of the figure now atop him.

Winded and unable to escape Morgan struggled with all of his strength. Morgan bit down on the wrist of the hand that was grasping at his throat. The man yelped and released his grip. Morgan pushed upwards as the man suddenly burst into flames and fell to the floor, rolling around in an attempt to extinguish the fire consuming his robe.

Morgan pulled himself to his feet and coughed violently. Mary stood before him, a candle in her still bound hands.

'I couldn't leave you,' she told him.

'Thank you,' he smiled momentarily before glimpsing four figures descending the crater behind her. Shirley was held between two cultists, with a third limping painfully behind them.

The other members of the conclave were also returning, and began to close in on Morgan and Mary from all directions. Morgan picked up the crowbar and held it tightly at his side. The two guards rose to their feet, one still rubbed his head, whilst the other shook himself out of the charred robe.

'You cannot stop the ceremony,' said a grave voice as the hooded figures surrounded them, 'chaos will always win.'

Morgan glanced at Mary and whispered, 'Run when I say run.'

She shot him a puzzled glance; his voice drowned out by a deafening hum as the candles on the altar were simultaneously extinguished.

A bright light suddenly filled the crater. Morgan looked up at the source, a police helicopter flying low directly above them. Lights sprung up all around them as figures in fluorescent jackets shone their heavy-duty torches over the rim of the crater, illuminating the bizarre scene below.

'They made it,' Morgan shouted over the din, 'The police made it.'

Twelve:

It took the rest of the night for the police to take Morgan's statement and, corroborating it with those of Mary and Shirley, let him go home. Eleven men and six women, including Julie, had been arrested and all the staff at Newton police station were busy trying to process paperwork and keep journalists at bay. Morgan was told to keep in touch as the information he could provide would be essential to building a solid case against the kidnappers.

Morgan slept soundly until the middle of Saturday afternoon. He sat in the garden with a cup of tea and some toast, revelling in the sunshine and fresh air after his two spells of captivity, the first in the back of the van and the second in a police interview room. Before long he was busy revisiting his aunt's research notes, the scrawled translation of *Al-Azif* and the other books she had been studying.

The revelations of the previous night shone new light on the information both he and his aunt had gathered and Morgan was able to draw a series of conclusions based on the evidence before him. Monksford, it seemed, had been a hot bed of the occult since the first meteorite landed in the Middle Ages. The practice of sacrificing a virgin on the altar had been wiped out by the witch trials, only to return upon the arrival of the second meteor. The cultists believed the age of chaos was approaching, when the ancient forces of evil would consume the world in a cleansing fire of disease, destruction and turmoil. They welcomed the changes the world would bring about, a so-called return to the old gods, and attempted to assist matters by performing their obscene rituals.

Morgan also found a previously unnoticed letter from Dr Zigler advising his aunt to read *Al-Azif* only in small doses. The professor had become quite insane but in his moments of lucidity, it seemed he had provided Aunt 'Liza with real insight into the meaning of the rituals performed by the disciples of chaos. Morgan resolved to return the book to the bank first thing on Monday morning, where it would be safe and no further harm could come to him from reading it.

That evening, Shirley came around and found him in the garden, once again perusing his aunt's notes. They made a pot of tea and sat on the bench in quiet contemplation for several long minutes, listening to the evening birdsong in the gentle summer breeze.

'What will you do now?' Shirley asked.

'Well, now that I have all the answers, I'm going to finish Aunt 'Liza's book and hopefully get my publishers interested.'

'Will you stay in Monksford?'
'For a little while, until the police have asked me all the questions they need to ask and then, I don't know. I think it might do to get away a while, I have friends in Bristol I can stay with while I write everything up.'
Shirley nodded, a sad look in her eyes.
'Don't worry. I'll stay in touch and I'll visit often.'
'You won't disappear again?'
'No. I promise I won't disappear again.'
The two friends lapsed back into quiet, Shirley resting her head gently on Morgan's shoulder.
'What about the cottage?' she asked.
'I don't know. I don't think I can face selling it but it would be a shame for it to sit empty.'
'You could rent it out?'
Morgan shifted uncomfortably, 'I don't know,' he replied, 'I don't like the idea of strangers living here.'
'I'll rent it from you,' Shirley suggested, 'The lease on my place is up soon and I've always loved this house. It means you'll have some money coming in and you know it will be in good hands.'
'That sounds like a good idea,' Morgan smiled, 'And I'd have a place to stay when I come and visit.'
    The two old friends chatted and laughed the evening away, reminiscing about old times, the adventures of the previous night and plans for the future. As the sun began to set behind the distant

hills and the evening grew cool, they lay on the grass and gazed at the stars as they faded into view. A speck of light flashed across the sky as a meteor burned up in the Earth's atmosphere.

'A shooting star,' Shirley declared, with childlike delight, 'Make a wish.'

Morgan smiled, closed his eyes against the tears and silently made his wish.

About the Author

Jon Matthews is a stand-up comedian and writer from Southampton, UK. He performs themed comedy and has been described as producing "punchlines you can feel smart for getting" (Chortle). He works for a homeless charity during the day and enjoys camping, hiking and kayaking with his wife, Liz.

Printed in Great Britain
by Amazon

43489207R00076